‹11S.

2015

Gant!

Gant!

LAURENCE TODD

THE CHOIR PRESS

First published in the United Kingdom in 2014 by
The Choir Press

ISBN 978-1-909300-34-7

ONE

Monday evening

THE TWO MEN were running for their lives down the street. Fast. They were scared, one of them absolutely terrified, and they had no idea where they were going to. They just knew what they were running from. Was this madman still behind them and where could they go to shake him off?

Ten minutes earlier they'd been coming out of a large multiplex cinema after seeing the last screening of a recent blockbuster. Both agreed that Spielberg was losing his touch and that the evening had been a waste of time and money. They should have gone to the club instead and seen if there were any women who might have taken their fancy. "That's the last time I let you talk me into going to see a Steven Spielberg film," the younger of the two said. His older brother slapped him around the side of his head, not quite playfully, and told him to shut the fuck up.

They walked along the main road then crossed over and turned left towards a piece of waste ground where they'd parked their stolen car. It had been easy to steal. Despite all the exhortations from police and insurance companies not to do so, many drivers still left their spare keys behind the visor above the steering wheel. All that was required was a Slim Jim to open the locked car, take the keys and drive away. The older one wondered whether the car owner would have the honesty to tell the insurance company he'd been complicit in the theft of his own vehicle.

"Come on, man, start the damn car, huh? Let's see if we can get a beer someplace, maybe meet some skirt so the evening won't be a complete waste."

Louis Phipps was talking to his younger brother, Paulie,

1

who was fumbling with the keys whilst trying to find the right one in the dark. Paulie, who had just turned 19, and a young 19, always tried his hardest to please his brother. Louis was his hero for all the wrong reasons. He took no kind of lip from anyone and lived for himself. Paulie was too weak and so in thrall to his brother's aura, he couldn't see that Louis had all the makings of a man destined either for a lifetime in prison or an early, possibly unmarked, grave because he'd crossed the wrong person at the wrong time.

Louis was almost 22 and already a career criminal. His crime sheet was impressively long, with convictions for assault, burglary, shoplifting and taking and driving away as well as being in possession of a small amount of a class B drug. He'd also appeared before the Magistrates' Court recently, charged and convicted of the stealing of a car and receiving a suspended sentence. He'd been warned he would go to prison if he appeared in court again anytime soon.

"Here it is," Paulie said triumphantly. He held the key up for Louis to see.

Both men heard the gunshots at the same time. A sound like "Phut" repeated a number of times in only a couple of seconds and the feel of bullets speeding past their heads and exploding against the old warehouse wall. They dropped to the ground.

"Christ, it's him. He's found us again. I thought you said we'd lost him."

Paulie was scared. That was evident in his quavering voice. He was lying on the floor, shaking. His breathing was erratic and he could feel his heartbeat racing at what felt like 200 miles an hour. Louis was angry but couldn't see far enough into the dark to focus his anger.

"Shut up, Paulie, I'm trying to think," Louis whispered harshly at his brother.

He looked in the direction the bullets had come from. It was dark and he couldn't see any signs of movement. There were bushes, a few trees and a number of other cars, plus an absence of street lighting – plenty of vantage points for a man with a gun to hide. He could be circling around trying to pick them off from the other side of the park. They had to get away or else be picked off like ripe cherries from a low hanging tree. He waited a few moments whilst his heartbeat stopped racing.

"We gotta get outa here, Paulie," Louis whispered.

"How we gonna do that, Louis?"

Louis looked around. Behind where they'd parked was a chain-link fence with a gap wide enough for an adult male to squeeze through. Beyond that was a side road leading away.

"Paulie, when I tell you, crawl over there to that fence." He nodded towards it. "Get through that gap and start running. I'll catch you up."

"Okay, Louis." The terror in his voice was noticeable.

Louis looked around. Now was as good a time as any.

"Go," Louis ordered his brother.

Paulie crouched down and ran towards the fence. He saw the gap and went through it. He was expecting to hear the sound of gunfire. He didn't. He started to run.

Louis waited a few moments then did the same. He scrambled through the fence remarkably nimbly as his sense of survival was much more greatly honed than Paulie's. Survival was what it had always been about for Louis Phipps. He began running and soon caught up with his brother.

"Where we going, Louis?" Paulie was gasping, already out of breath.

"Just keep running. Let's get away from this fucking madman."

She could feel the car lurching slightly to the right and she could hear the dull sound, almost a schlopping type sound, the sound a tyre makes when it's going down and the car is beginning to run on the front axle. She knew she had a puncture in the front tyre. She navigated the car to the side of the road and stopped. Damn. She was only two miles from home as well. Her boyfriend would be wondering where she was. She couldn't see a phone box and her mobile was out of battery power so she couldn't call and ask him to drive over and help her change the tyre, and she didn't have enough money for a taxi.

Amanda Redmond had had the car, a graphite blue Mini, bought for her by her father as a congratulations present for getting all grade As plus one A* in her A level exams the previous summer, which had meant her getting a place at university in London. She'd passed her driving test first time and had taken to the Mini in the same easy manner a baby duck takes to the water. This was the first thing that had gone wrong with the car. She knew there was a spare tyre in the boot but didn't think she was strong enough to undo the nuts holding the punctured tyre on. She needed help.

Looking along the darkened street she could see the sign that indicated there was a bar open. She decided to ask for help there. Bound to be a man in there who could help me change the tyre, she thought to herself. She locked the car door and walked along the road to the bar. As she arrived at the steps leading down to the entrance, two men came out. They both nodded to her, with one holding the door open for her. She briefly wondered whether to ask one of those but, as she got to the door, the man smiled and walked away. She continued into the bar.

Louis and Paulie were now a few roads away from where they'd left their car.

"Have we lost him yet, Louis?" Paulie was breathing hard and his pace was slowing. He was not a fit man.

"Hell do I know?" Louis shouted. "We gotta get off the road and find a place to lie low for a while. Hey look, over there. Paulie, come on."

They crossed the road.

Amanda looked around the bar. There were only two people there and neither were customers. A woman was sweeping the floor and there was a man behind the counter wiping some glasses and stacking them in neat rows next to the till. It was not very big, maybe eighty feet long and about half as wide, with an alcove in the corner by the toilet door. There was an illuminated sign for the toilets and several pictures around the walls of famous sporting personalities, like footballers and rugby players, and the occasional boxer. The bar did not look at all salubrious and she was glad her boyfriend would never even consider bringing her to a place like this. It had the feel and smell of the kind of place men went to when they didn't want to be alone at night.

"We're just closing. Can I help you?" The man behind the counter asked.

Mickey Corsley had run the bar since he'd opened it after leaving the police a few years back, which he'd joined after six years in the army. He was 33 and looked younger. He'd left the army because he'd twice tried and failed to join the SAS and, as he was not considered 'Officer and Gentleman' material, to quote one of his commanding officers, Mickey had decided to join the police. He also helped out at a local sports centre giving classes in self-defence to teenagers and others who wanted to be able to protect themselves.

"Oh, ah, yes. My car's got a puncture and I was wondering if there was anybody here who could help me change a flat tyre."

"Sounds like a job for you, Sir Galahad," Sarah Corsley said with a smile. She was Mickey's wife and the co-manager of the bar. They'd been married six years and she'd been all in favour of Mickey leaving uniformed service and going into the entertainment business, as she referred to running a pub, albeit on a small scale.

"Where you parked?" Mickey asked.

"Just along the road outside, right down the far end."

"I'll finish up here. You help the young lady," Sarah said.

Mickey came around from behind the bar. At that

moment the front doors crashed open and two men came running into the bar. Both were carrying small handguns. Mickey's initial concern was that he was the wrong side of the bar. He had a cosh, a sap and also a small handgun behind the counter but they were in the cabinet beneath the glasses shelf and it was locked.

"What the hell—" Mickey began to say.

"Shut it, just shut it. Alright?" the older of the two men shouted as he pointed his gun at Mickey.

He looked around. There were only three people, and two of them looked like they were getting ready to leave.

"Real popular joint this, isn't it?" Louis Phipps laughed.

"Closing time, pal. That's why no one's here."

Mickey could feel the anger rising within him but he'd been trained to be calm and rational in these kinds of situation and wait for the right moment. This wasn't it.

"Paulie, lock those doors."

Paulie nodded. He closed both the doors to the bar and slid the bolt above the main door into place and flipped the catch on the Yale lock. They were now locked in.

Mickey's initial thought was that the two men were intending to rob them, but locking the doors meant they weren't planning on leaving just yet. What was going on?

"Who's the manager of this dump?" Louis Phipps asked.

"That'd be me, and it's not a dump, okay?" Mickey said calmly.

"Yeah, whatever. You got a back exit here?"

"Nope."

"What do you mean, no?"

"Exactly what it means, there's no back exit. That's the only way in or out of here," Mickey nodded at the front door, "and you've just locked it."

"You got an upstairs here, anywhere above this place?"

"There is but it isn't ours. We just have the ground floor. We can't get upstairs from here even if we wanted to. There's no access from here."

"And there's no back rooms or any other way out?"

"You got it."

"Jesus," Louis sighed. This wasn't what he'd expected. He'd thought he'd go into the bar and leave through the back way, throwing their pursuer off the scent. It hadn't worked. The realisation dawned on him he may be trapped with a maniac waiting for him outside. He tried to compose himself and think. To go back outside was to invite this maniac to shoot at them again, possibly even killing them in the process. The man might not be able to find them but he didn't want to take a chance on that. He'd already found them again this evening.

"What're we going to do, Louis?" Paulie asked, imploring his brother to have the right answer.

"For the moment, we're gonna stay put. Not much else we can do."

Paulie shrugged and shook his head.

"Okay, you two, sit over there, against the wall."

Louis pointed his gun between Mickey and Sarah. Mickey looked at Sarah and raised his eyebrows, a gesture which she knew meant to go along with the situation and keep calm. I'll get us out of this. They walked over to the wall, next to the pool table, and took a chair each and sat down.

"Paulie, watch them. Think you can do that?"

Paulie nodded and walked across to where the Corsleys sat. He sat a few feet away and pointed his gun at them. Mickey could see the younger of the two men was scared. That much was evident from the look in his eyes. He was holding the gun with all the bravura of someone holding the business end of an anaconda. Mickey thought that, if he could just get close enough, he could take the man's gun away and clean his teeth for him with it, but he wasn't going to risk the life of his wife and an innocent teenage girl who was only in the bar wanting a tyre changing.

Paulie took off his jacket. His green T-shirt had sweat stains under the armpits and across his chest from the exertion of running. Mickey could see Paulie's arms. They were thin and had no defined muscle tone. Piece of cake to take this wimp, he thought.

Louis Phipps walked to the counter and sat on a barstool. He unbuttoned his shirt collar and loosened his tie. He was breathing less heavily now.

"Hey, sweetheart, come on over here." He was looking at Amanda Redmond.

"Alright, but tell this guy not to shoot me when I get up," Mickey said. Sarah laughed.

"You a wiseguy or something?" Louis snarled at him.

"Or something. I've been called worse things."

"You get out that chair and I'll blow out one of your fucking kneecaps." He turned back to Amanda. "Come on, honey, over here."

Amanda was scared but she walked across to where Louis Phipps sat. She stood in front of him.

"What's your name, sweetheart? "

"Amanda," she replied quietly.

"Amanda, that's a nice name. Tell you what, honey, you play your cards right, you and me might get better acquainted before the night's over."

His smile had the same menace a lion has when it spots a helpless deer grazing twenty yards away. He turned her around so she was facing Mickey and Sarah and he pulled her closer. He put his left arm around her shoulder, still holding the gun. His right hand was holding a particularly vicious looking knife, which he was tapping against his thigh in time to music only he could hear.

"Hey, hotshot," Louis called to Mickey, "If that door there's the only way in or out, where do you get all your beer delivered to?"

"Just along the road. There's a cellar entrance where barrels and crates get lowered into. We hook it up to the pumps and it comes up through the pipes on the bar. Spirits, crisps and other snacks get delivered through the front door."

"No other way out through there, I suppose."

"Nope. That's why it's called a cellar."

Louis looked around and shook his head. He was thinking about his situation.

It began to dawn on Mickey that these men had planned to come in through the front and go out through a back entrance, but hadn't bargained on there being no back exit. They were as much a prisoner as he was.

"If you're planning to rob us, pal, you're out of luck. I cashed up a little while back and the money's down the tube. You can't get at it."

"Down the tube?"

"Yeah, it's a security procedure. Lots of small businesses round here use something similar. The till gets cashed up and all the notes and coins go into a bank bag and dropped down this little vault. Only way to get at it is with a key from the bank."

"Actually, no, I wasn't planning on that at all, I mean, does this dump have anything worth stealing? It does look like a real classy joint, doesn't it?" he said sarcastically.

"If you're not going to rob us, why are you here? What have we done to deserve your sparkling company this time of night?" He ignored the slight on his bar.

"We're trying to get away from someone," Paulie Phipps opined.

"Paulie, shut up, will you?" Louis raised his voice.

"There's someone out there trying to kill us." The panic showed in Paulie's voice.

"Now my brother's taken you into our confidence," Louis spat out his invective at his brother, "he's right. Some fucking nutter outside is taking shots at us. That's why we came into here."

Mickey resisted the desire to offer congratulations to whoever it was.

"What, just like that?"

"Yeah, I've no idea why this guy keeps shooting at us."

"You sure about that? No one just starts shooting at someone for no reason. You've obviously upset the wrong person somewhere."

"Told you, man, we ain't done nothing." Louis sounded angry.

"So, you're in a trap, so to speak," Mickey said.

Neither man replied.

"If you need it, I can show you a possible way out of this mess."

"Oh yeah, how?" Louis sneered.

I was at home in Acton, in the flat I shared with my partner, Karen, lying on the couch and reading a book about Britain in the 1950s, a decade I was endlessly fascinated by. I was currently on a week's holiday from my job as a DS in the Special Branch and was enjoying the break as it was going to be a chance to catch up on my reading.

Which was why I was annoyed when the phone rang just after 10.45pm. I was engrossed in my book and did not want to be disturbed as I had another chapter to finish before bedtime. I decided not to answer. I had an answerphone; whoever it was could leave a message. I kept reading.

"Evening, Rob, sorry to disturb you at this late hour but there's some fun here. Pick up if you're in." It was Mickey.

The phrase 'there's some fun here' was code for 'there's a situation here and I need your help'. I picked up.

"Mr Corsley, what time do you call this?" I said, mock seriously.

"Apologies, but as I said, there's some fun here, can you come to the bar?"

"On my way."

I'd known Mickey for a few years. I knew him when he was a rookie police constable after he'd left the army about seven years ago. I was still based at West End Central, as was he, and he'd been with me on a few occasions when warrants for arrests were being served on reluctant criminals. I'd been sort of, but not completely, surprised when he'd quit after only a few years to open a bar in Bayswater. But we'd kept in touch and were friends.

Mickey's Bar, as it was unimaginatively named, was just off Inverness Terrace, close to Bayswater Tube station. I could understand his desire to open his own bar but quite why he'd chosen such a tacky location was something I didn't understand.

I drove to the bar and parked outside. I looked around. The street was dark and there were few people around. Out the corner of my eye I thought I saw a slight movement at the entrance to the alleyway opposite but I wasn't sure. I couldn't see anything in the dark.

I approached the doors, tried opening them but found them locked. I knocked and stepped back. Mickey opened them. His eyes quickly darted right. I nodded. If there was anyone waiting, that would be the obvious place to hide. I entered.

A man appeared behind me, holding a small handgun as he bolted the door. He looked to be about 18 or 19 and seemed unsure of himself. He was physically unimposing and, had the chance arisen, Mickey could have made a reef knot out of him.

"Search him, Paulie," a voice called from the other side of the room.

I could see someone sitting on a barstool with a young girl in front of him. Were they partners in whatever was going down? Paulie patted the pockets of my jacket and my jeans. That was the extent of my frisking. I've been searched more thoroughly by pets looking for treats.

"He's clean, Louis," the man called out to the other one at the bar. I actually was clean but, had I known this clown was here, I'd have hidden a weapon. I could probably have snuck a bazooka in past this idiot. If he was the brains behind whatever was going on here, God help them.

Paulie gestured to Mickey to return to his seat. I saw Sarah sitting in the corner by the pool table. I nodded and smiled. She returned it. Mickey sat next to her and Gunman sat nearby pointing his gun at them.

"Hey you, over here."

I walked towards the bar. I could see a young girl standing in front of someone sitting on a barstool and, if I'd originally thought they were partners, I was proved wrong. She looked scared and unsure of what to do. She had her arms folded across her breasts as though she was protecting herself.

The man sitting behind her was a wholly different proposition from the man at the door. He looked like the other guy so my guess was they were brothers. He looked to be in his early twenties and, like the guy at the door, looked Mediterranean with a thick shock of black curly hair. But it was his eyes I particularly noticed. Whereas the guy at the door had eyes that showed how scared he was, this guy had almost impenetrably deep eyes, betraying a sense of unfeeling, as though he'd kill without a second's hesitation. The kind of eyes that suggested he'd put a cat in a microwave just to see what would happen next. That, combined with the nasty looking knife in his left hand, suggested it would be important not to get him too worked up. I didn't doubt he was a psychopath.

I stood a few feet from him. I looked at the girl and nodded.

"Don't be scared, lady, he'll not harm you while I'm here." I tried to sound reassuring. The man behind her fixed me with what I assumed he thought was a hard stare.

"You the guy he told us about?" He jutted his chin towards Mickey.

My usual response would be some kind of flippancy, something like "No, I'm Hansel, I'm sorry Gretel couldn't make it," but I didn't want to get this guy irate so soon. He probably thought flippancy was the act of using flippers.

"Yeah, I am. Who might you be?"

"Straight down to business. I like that. Your name's McGraw, isn't it?"

"It is. DS McGraw, Special Branch. Like I said, who might you be?"

He looked at me for a few moments, sizing me up, wondering whether I was able to help him.

"Name's Louis Phipps. Okay, here's the deal. There's a madman out there trying to kill my brother and I, and I want you to go out there and stop him."

Brothers. I was right. That might explain the movement I thought I'd seen by the alleyway. Maybe the guy wasn't as paranoid as I'd thought.

"What, just like that? I'm to go out into a dark street and take on someone I don't know, in an environment I'm unfamiliar with, and do it whilst unarmed?" I stated flatly. "What do you want me to do exactly, ask him nicely to leave you alone?"

"Don't be a smartarse, this is serious. There's someone out there taking shots at me and Paulie and I want you to get rid of him."

"Look, just calm down. Before I do anything, I want to know exactly what's happening here, so start at the beginning. In words of one syllable, so I can understand it, tell me what's going on. If, as you say, there's someone on your tail, why is this the case?"

"I don't know, man, we ain't done nothing."

"Well, if that's the case, why not go to the police and report it to them? People firing guns indiscriminately is a serious matter.

"No police, you got that? No fucking police." He pointed at me with his knifehand and raised his voice, which caused the young girl to scream. "Fucking police have got me in enough trouble already, I don't want no fucking more."

"Okay, okay, just calm down." I made a patting gesture with my hands. I looked at the girl. "Take it easy, you're safe while I'm here." She nodded. She looked scared. I took a deep breath. "Right, now I've ascertained you and your brother are vestal virgins and free from the stain of original sin, as I just said, start from the beginning. Why is this gentleman outside after you? Did he just pull your names out of a hat or what?"

The man put the knife on the counter of the bar.

"It started just recently. Paulie and I were in a pub the other night—"

"Which one and where?" I interrupted him.

"In Brixton, near where we live, place called the Barn Door."

I nodded. "Okay, continue."

"We was just having a drink in this pub when some bloke calmly strolls over to our table and says that we should enjoy our drinks as he's going to kill us both pretty soon, then he turns and walks away. I jumped up and chased after him as he walked out the door, but he'd vanished, I couldn't see him anywhere. I didn't think anyone could disappear that quick. Anyway, I thought he was just some fucking nutjob so I ignored it. Later on, we're going home and that same person appears the other side of the road and fires at us. We run for it. He shot at us again a couple of nights back, this time near our place in Brixton. We managed to give him the slip, stayed at a friend's place for a couple of nights, but earlier this evening he appears again as we're getting into our car and takes a pop at us. We run for it and we end up in this dive."

"Sounds like you've had a fun-filled few nights," I said alliteratively.

"Fuck fun-filled, I'm sick of this guy shooting at us. I want you to stop him."

I thought for a few moments. The urge to kill this guy and his dumb brother was understandable but it didn't make sense as it stood. Whoever was shooting at them was clearly not very proficient, unless there was a more devious agenda involved.

"And you still maintain you've no idea why whoever it is is shooting at you?"

"That's right, I don't."

"Okay, take a step back. You're in the pub and some guy just comes up and announces your impending demise. Who was this person? Had you ever seen him before? Describe him. What does he look like?"

"Probably about your height, six foot or so, sounded American, wore a trilby or some kind of hat and a combat jacket, sort of a military jacket type thing. I think he had a scar by his nose."

"Left side of his nose?"

"Yeah, it was."

I was getting an uncomfortable feeling I knew who he was describing.

"Did he say what his name was?"

"Yeah, called himself something like Gant."

I breathed out. I smiled and shook my head. I looked around at Mickey. He mouthed, "He did say Gant, didn't he?" I nodded.

"What you two talking about? What's so funny?" Louis was agitated.

"It's not so much funny as, ah . . ." I paused. "Do you want to tell him, Mickey?"

He was grinning. "Nah, it'd sound better coming from you." I turned back to Knifeman.

"It's not so much funny, just that you don't seem to pick your enemies particularly well, do you?"

I said this slowly for greater impact. "You have a poor choice of enemy."

"What, you know this guy?" He sounded almost optimistic.

"I know of him. If it's the same Gant I know about, he's a top class contract man."

"A what?"

"Oh, come on, sonny, it means he's an assassin, a hired

gun. He's a paid killer, that's what he is, one of the best in the world. If it's the same one, I can't believe you're still breathing if he's taken as many shots at you as you say he has."

Louis appeared unhappy at that comment.

"How do you know this guy? Does he work for you?" he asked.

"No," I shook my head. "He's a freelance killer. Works for anyone who can afford his services, and they don't come cheap either. You know what this suggests? There's someone out there who wants you dead very much if they're prepared to pay someone like Gant to come after you. So, you better have a rethink, sonny. *Why* is Gant after you?

I knew Gant by reputation. He was what was known as a person of interest to the security services and his every visit to the country would be logged and noted. I knew a few things about him. I knew he'd been in the first Iraq war, operating behind enemy lines as a sniper and had left the army to join the CIA and engage in covert activities before going freelance. He was rumoured to have killed a top British industrialist suspected of leaking secret information about germ warfare testing at Porton Down, but this was never conclusively proven. People like Gant were used to do the dirty jobs Government wanted to be able to deny. How did that square with his pursuing people like these two? It didn't make sense.

Actually, I went on, "I'm wondering what someone like *you* could have done to get a top notch hitman like him after you. I don't know Gant but I know the kind of work he does and the kind of people he kills and, frankly, you don't fit the bill."

"What might that mean?" He looked annoyed.

"His usual targets are enemies of the state – spies, traitors, people like that. As I said, I know a few things about Gant. You're right, he is American. You know who the Green Berets are?"

"No."

"They're the American equivalent of the SAS, the elite soldiers of their respective armies. Gant was one of the best. He's an expert with guns, with knives, with his bare hands in unarmed combat. He's a crack marksman. He can shoot the tits off a queen bee from 500 yards away firing into a head wind. During the first Iraq war, Desert Storm, he was seconded into the CIA and worked as a sniper behind enemy lines taking out key Iraqi military personnel, and he was damn good at it. Afterwards, he left the army and went freelance, and he gets used by governments or others who want someone taken out of the equation but with maximum deniability. As I said, he's a top class hitman, which is why I can't understand why you two are still breathing good air."

Phipps stared at me for about six seconds, wondering about the veracity of what he'd just been told and whether to believe me.

"How do you know all this? You just trying to scare me?" He looked like he'd just heard worse than expected news from the doctor.

"No. When I first heard about this character, I checked him out. He's known to the security services in this country because of what he does, so that means every time he sets foot in the UK, a watch is kept on him. Trust me, from what I've seen, his rep is well earned. I'm not trying to scare you, simply outlining to you who it is who might be outside that door waiting to greet you with a bullet. If it really is Gant out there, you two have chance against him." The *no* was emphasised.

If my intent had been to irritate Louis Phipps, I was succeeding. He was looking very uncomfortable at what he'd heard, his brother even more so.

"Oh, God, Louis, we've got Rambo after us. We can't take him on." Either Paulie had developed a sudden cold or he was trying not to cry. It sounded pitiful.

"Just shut it, Paulie, eh? I'm trying to think."

He closed his eyes for a few seconds. I briefly considered jumping him but the presence of his brother behind me, armed and irrational with fear and who might just fire blindly and kill the girl, or, even worse, me, persuaded me not to.

"Look, you want me to get rid of this guy, if he's out there. Okay, I'll go outside and see if he's there. If he is, I'll try and talk to him, see what this is all about."

"What, you mean arrest him?"

"Don't be stupid, pal," I said flatly. "People like Gant are beyond arrest. They work for national governments. You know what that means? It means he knows where the bodies are buried, so to speak, which is appropriate for Gant as he probably put most of them there."

I smiled at Mickey. He nodded. "Nice one. You're a funny guy, Rob."

Louis Phipps hadn't seen the joke. He looked as though he wanted to lash out at something or someone. Time to calm him down.

"No, I'm not going to arrest him. What could I arrest him for anyway? I'm simply going to try and find out what this is all about. I couldn't arrest him even if I wanted to. I've no evidence he's done anything, have I, only the word of two frankly quite unreliable witnesses. So I'm just going to talk to him. Maybe all this can be resolved without anyone dying, though in Gant's world people often do that." I grinned at him.

The look on Phipps' face suggested he didn't believe me.

"I give you my word I'll just try and talk to this guy. I'll come straight back in afterwards. I don't want anyone dying any more than you do." I turned to Mickey. "You still have the same number on your Blackberry?"

"Yeah."

"I'll call when I'm coming back in. Meanwhile, when I'm outside, keep the doors locked and stay away from the windows. If he is out there and decides he's fed up with target practice, he may just decide it's time to play for keeps."

Phipps looked doubtful at everything I'd just said.

"This is the only choice you got, pal. As things stand, I'm probably the only thing keeping you two from an early grave."

I turned and walked towards the door.

"This better not be a trick on your part, mate. Don't forget I've got three hostages in here." Phipps called out as Paulie opened the door for me.

"Yeah," I replied semi-facetiously, "so you have."

"Do what you can, mister." Paulie looked at me almost longingly. He had the expression of someone who'd just been told that potentially life-saving surgery had been cancelled. He shut the door as I stepped outside and I heard the bolts sliding back into place. They were locked inside with no way out and a triple 'A' assassin waiting for them outside. If it was him.

I walked to my car and looked around. The street was almost deserted, with a car passing by and a taxi waiting for a pick-up outside a house further down the road. Most premises along the street were in darkness. Other than Mickey's bar, all other businesses were shut for the evening.

A pencil-thin red beam hit me in the chest and, for a second, made me jump. I looked across the road to the source of the beam. I could see a shape in the dark holding a gun of some kind and pointing it in my direction.

"Follow the light," an American voice called out.

The beam dropped down the road and went backwards. I followed it across the road and into an alleyway. About twenty yards along, near to a street light at the end by the road parallel, a man was standing. He switched the beam off.

"You're Robert McGraw, a Special Branch DS. Am I right?"

I was surprised he knew who I was.

"Yeah. How did you know that?"

"I saw you go into the bar and I gave your description to

someone who checked you out. He said, from the description, it was almost certainly you as you're known to be friends with the guy who runs the place. Someone called Corsley?"

Who might Gant know who knew me well enough to match the description given?

"I know Mickey. You must be Phil Gant."

"Louis tell you that, did he?" He smirked.

"Amongst other things."

"Let me guess. You're here because you want to know why I'm on the trail of those two losers in the bar, the Phipps brothers. That right?"

"Pretty much," I agreed. "I don't know you but I know something about the kind of work you do, and I know those two in the bar are nothing like the targets you usually get paid to go after. It just doesn't make sense that someone like you is after them."

"Lots of things don't make sense, man. People like me get paid to make sense of them."

He was smiling as he spoke. Was that a good thing? A smile from Gant would usually be the equivalent of seeing a tiger smiling whilst looking at a potential dinner walking innocently along. People like Gant will smile with you one second and put a bullet between your eyes the next.

"But, if you're Special Branch, you'll know something about the kind of world I live and work in. The one thing I bet you *do* know is that, when someone like myself is hired to do a job of work, shall we say," he looked straight at me, "the transaction is confidential. Whoever it is who's hired me would not want personal details being made public."

"That's true, but it doesn't change the situation. I don't like the idea of foreign mercenaries playing *Assassin's Creed* in our country, and especially not here in London, even if you are someone who's worked for governments both sides of the Atlantic. Anyway, you still haven't told me why someone with your rep is going after the Phipps brothers.

They told me you'd already taken shots at them and missed. If only a small part of what I hear about you is true, I can't believe you've missed a couple of times."

"Wasn't trying to kill them then, just trying to scare the shit outa them, make them panic, make them too afraid to leave home, then at a convenient time dispatch them to the afterlife any way I see fit. I got nothing else on at present and I'm road-testing a new gun, so I'm just having a little fun with them before I terminate their existence," he said, matter-of-factly.

I looked at the weapon in his hand. "What kind of gun is that?"

"It's a kind of variation of a Beretta 92 Centurion, specially adapted by some Israeli guy I know. Got a couple of special features like the red beam I used to attract your attention. Great for focusing on targets in the dark. I'm sort of road testing it for him on live targets but I'm not sure I like it all that much. I prefer my Sig Mauser."

I looked at him for a couple of moments.

"You do know the Phipps have got a couple of hostages in there, don't you? There's no way out other than that door there," I nodded across the road, "and the older of the two brothers is sufficiently reckless to start shooting blindly and kill everyone if he thinks he's trapped."

"I suspected there were a few others in there, that's why I haven't tried entering the place. I knew there wasn't a back way out. My contact confirmed that when I told him where I was."

"So, you going to wait out here all night?" I asked.

"What do you suggest?"

"You turn around and leave. Defuse the situation. Defuse that maniac in there who's holding a knife at a young girl's throat. I've no evidence you've committed anything I could take you in for, only the word of someone like Louis Phipps, and that's probably as reliable as a dog in heat. So, why don't you just leave? There's nothing for you here."

Gant started to smile, then he laughed. Not raucously, but sufficient to slightly unnerve me. Was he laughing *at* me? At my suggestion he stop doing what he was doing? Or at my nerve in telling a top-notch assassin his target is off limits? It was hard to tell.

"They said you were a piece of work," he finally said.

"Who did?"

"Person who said it was probably you when I described who went into that place."

He paused and his face took on a serious expression.

"I don't actually give a rat's ass about this job, to be honest with you. I only took it on as a favour to someone I know, who offered me a ridiculous sum to kill those two assholes. As I said, I've got nothing else lined up and it gives me a chance to test this baby out." He held up the gun. "I'm just using this to keep my hand in. I'll tell you what . . ." He slid the gun into a shoulder holster and buttoned his jacket. "They may well die but it won't be tonight, alright? It's late, I'm tired and I'm gonna go back to my hotel. So, tell Phipps he's off the hook tonight. A pair like them will be easy to find, like finding sand on a beach." He nodded at me.

"You still haven't told me what they've done to attract the attention of someone like you. Who'd want them dead that badly they'll pay what you charge?"

"You'd be surprised. Take care, Robert."

Gant patted me on the arm, turned and walked away and, at the end of the alleyway, turned left and disappeared.

I walked back to the bar. The lights had been dimmed and I couldn't see any shapes through the window. I knocked on the door.

"That you, Rob?" Mickey called out a few seconds later.

"Yeah. I'm alone."

The door opened. Mickey stepped back. Paulie Phipps appeared, still holding a gun.

"Come on, inside quickly." He still sounded nervous.

I entered. Paulie stepped forward to lock the doors. In his haste he'd forgotten about telling us both to move away whilst he did so. A very basic error. Mickey jumped forward and grabbed Paulie's gunhand, twisting the wrist around with his left hand whilst his right hand snatched the gun from Paulie's grasp. He spun Paulie around and headbutted him. Paulie dropped to the floor, hands to his face and moaning from the pain.

Louis realised what was happening a second too late. By the time he was aware of the changed situation, Paulie had been neutralised. He looked worried. Mickey was holding Paulie's gun. Louis raised the knife and placed it next to Amanda's throat. She screamed as he gripped her tightly.

"Stay back or I'll slice her," he shouted.

"Think about it, huh? Look around. There's two of us, Louis, you'll not get past us both. Just put the knife down, okay? Nobody gets hurt that way." I said this calmly but authoritatively.

Louis looked around as though seeking a way out. But the only exit was the front door, and Mickey and I were standing by it. His chances of winning the lottery were better than his getting past us. Mickey was armed. He started to move away from me. Phipps was looking between the two of us, wondering who was going to make a grab for him.

After a stand-off lasting close to a minute, Phipps' resolve broke.

"Okay, okay." He released Amanda and she moved away from him. Phipps put the knife on the counter and raised his hands slightly. Mickey and I approached the bar.

"Go sit over there, lady," Mickey said to Amanda, nodding towards Sarah. She did. Sarah put her arm around Amanda's shoulder. She was trembling, rubbing her eyes and trying not to cry.

"You're safe now, everything's fine," Sarah said reassuringly. Amanda nodded, wiping a couple of tears from her cheeks.

Mickey took Phipps' knife and looked at it admiringly. I put his gun in my jacket pocket.

"Impressive," I said. "You know how many years in prison carrying this means? Doesn't matter that you had no intent to use it, just having it on your person means prison. If you've got a record, and I'll bet you have, sentence can be even longer. You ready to do time, Louis?"

Phipps said nothing. He looked deflated. The cold arrogance in his eyes had temporarily evaporated. He was helpless and he knew it. There was no longer any certainty of his status. The swaggering bully of a few moments ago was in limbo.

"I'm going to take these two to West End Central and talk to them there, find out what's going on."

I turned to face a very dejected Louis Phipps. Mickey walked to the door and helped a dazed and very confused Paulie Phipps to his feet. He was holding his face gingerly.

"C'mon, pal, this way."

Mickey guided Paulie to the bar. Paulie sat down.

"I'm sorry, Louis," Paulie said quietly, not looking at his brother.

"S'okay, Paulie. I know you're a prize fuck-up." Louis looked menacingly at his younger brother. Had Mickey and I not been present, I suspect Paulie would be getting a kicking about now.

"I'm taking you two in for questioning. For the moment you're not under arrest and I'm not going to cuff you, but either of you give me cause to and I'll put bracelets on both of you, and I'll make it hurt. Got it?" I enjoyed saying that.

"Okay," Paulie said. He was rubbing the bruise on his forehead caused by meeting Mickey head on. Louis just stared straight ahead at something only he could see.

"I'll change the tyre for her then come with you," Mickey said.

Amanda Redmond was now looking a little more relaxed.

The immediate fear of violence from Louis Phipps had receded. She and Sarah came over to the bar.

"Thank you," she said softly. I nodded.

"Give Mickey your contact details, we may well need to talk to you again when this is over."

She agreed she would. Thanking me again she left the bar with Mickey. I was stuck with the handsome twins. I looked at the forlorn figure that was Paulie.

"How's your head?"

"Bit sore. Your friend's got a hard head." He rubbed the bruise again.

"That's 'cause he's thick." I smiled at him.

"Don't fucking talk to him. What are you, his best fucking friend all of a sudden?" Louis snapped. The old meanness and belligerence had returned. Paulie looked scared.

"Sorry Louis, I didn't mean anything by it."

"Shut your mouth, Phipps," I said quite aggressively and stood up. I wanted to kick the shit out of him. The thought of seeing his bloodied face minus some teeth on the floor was a delightful one but I resisted the temptation. "Be quiet or I'll gag you and make you stand in the corner facing the wall."

Louis stared at me for a moment, then went back to looking at whatever was holding his attention on the far wall.

Mickey returned after changing Amanda's car tyre. He washed his hands in the small sink behind the bar and then came and stood next to me.

"We taking your car?"

I nodded. "Yeah."

"I'll sit in the back with him," he jutted his chin at Paulie. "You can have braindead there in the front seat, though I'd watch him, if I were you. He looks fruity to me, looks like he'll make a move on your manhood you give him half a chance." Mickey laughed.

"Bastard," Phipps shouted.

He leapt at Mickey. Mickey stepped aside as Phipps threw a punch at him. He grabbed Mickey's jersey. Mickey broke his grip, almost contemptuously, with a chopping movement using both hands and put a hard right into Phipps' stomach. Louis dropped to his knees and remained on all fours, coughing and wheezing. He spat something out onto the floor. I helped him up and sat him on a barstool. He was still doubled up. For the moment the fight had left him.

"I'll bring the car forward."

I went out to my car. I put it into reverse and went back about twenty metres and stopped outside the doors. I kept the engine running. I went into the bar.

"Come on, gents, this way," Mickey said to the Phipps. Both got up and walked towards the doors.

"You, get in the back," he said to Paulie. Paulie nodded his assent. He was just glad to be leaving a bad situation behind him.

"I'll close up and go home," Sarah said to Mickey. He agreed it was a good idea.

I went in front and walked up the steps to the pavement. Paulie followed behind. Mickey steered Louis in front of him, alert and ready for him to do anything stupid. When we were all outside, Sarah closed the doors and went back inside to clear up before finally closing up after what had been an unexpectedly eventful night.

"You ready, Mickey?" I looked around the deserted street.

Two shots then rang out. I heard two "Phwew" type sounds from bullets fired from a gun with a silencer attached. Both Louis and Paulie Phipps dropped to the pavement. Both were dead. Louis had been hit in the heart, Paulie through his forehead. Killing both the Phipps brothers had taken less than one second.

Mickey and I had dropped at the first sound but neither of us could do anything to stop what happened. I crouched against my car and looked around. Where had the shots come from? Mickey had assumed a prone position and was scanning the immediate vicinity. He was holding Paulie's gun but had no idea which way to point it or who to shoot at. Between us we saw nothing. Neither of us knew where the shots had come from. However, I knew who it was who'd fired them.

Gant.

TWO

Tuesday

A FTER A NIGHT in which sleep had played no part at all, I was in my boss's office looking out over at St James's Park. My boss was DCI Jack Smitherman and he was looking at the report I'd written up after the events of the previous evening. I'd returned home and typed up what had occurred whilst the memory was still fresh.

His office was small but deceptively spacious. There were books on a shelf and a filing cabinet next to a table by the far wall. His overcoat was hanging from a hook behind the door. The walls had been painted white, giving the room an austere and utilitarian feel. Smitherman was sitting at his desk, looking relaxed and assured, with his laptop open but not being used.

When I'd been satisfied that whoever it was who'd pulled the trigger on the brothers had probably long since left the scene, Mickey had alerted the police. An ambulance also arrived to take away the dead bodies of the Phipps brothers. Two squad cars had arrived and I identified myself as a DS in Special Branch, and Mickey as the person who'd been with me, to the senior officer, DI Harrow. He and I had gone inside and I'd told him all about what had occurred that evening, from the time of the Phipps' arriving in the bar, the circumstances they'd said had led them there and ending with them prostrate on the pavement. I mentioned going outside the bar and talking to someone named Phil Gant, who had seemingly left the area after our little chat, and also my suspicion, given Gant's line of work, that he was involved in the deaths of the Phipps brothers. Paulie's gun had been checked and found not to have been fired. Louis's gun was in my jacket and also hadn't been fired. The DI taking Mickey's and my statements seemed satisfied with the sequence of events and our lack of any direct involvement with the dead bodies and had left after assuring me I didn't appear to be a prime suspect. Nice of him. DI Harrow said they'd be in touch again and they left after both dead bodies had been removed.

"Well, you certainly know how to enjoy a holiday, don't you?" Smitherman finally said. "Dead bodies cropping up everywhere. I thought you were going to take it easy."

"I'd not counted on running into a killer like Phil Gant."

"How are you feeling after being near the shootings? You okay? Do you need to talk to someone about what happened?"

"No, I'm alright, sir. It's not the first shooting scene I've been at. I don't need to talk to the house shrink. I'm fine."

He nodded. "Your report claims Phil Gant was the trigger-man."

"That's right, I'm convinced he was."

"You spoke to him not belong before the Phipps were shot," he stated.

"Yeah. I went out the bar to see if it was Gant that was after those two, as they'd said, and it was. I had a brief chat with him but didn't pick up anything, though he did confirm he was after the brothers. I asked him why but drew a blank."

"He knew you, though."

"So it seems. He saw me enter the bar, phoned someone with a description and it came back as me. He knows someone who knows me. Who that could be?" I mused.

"Maybe your pal over at *Prevental*?" He grinned at me.

This was a reference to Gavin Dennison, who'd been my assigned training officer when I'd first joined the Met from university. We were never close friends but we'd kept in touch and, from time to time after moving from CID to Special Branch, we'd swap notes, or rather I'd pick his brains about something I was stymied about. Which was quite often.

I'd not seen Gavin for a few months, not since I'd become convinced he was somehow involved in a case where three people who in one way or another had been involved with a Government-appointed committee investigating suspected paedophile activity in the Catholic Church had turned up dead. The suspected killer had been identified but he'd returned to Eire and had disappeared. The Irish police had been asked for all the details they had about someone named Martin Riley, travelling under the alias Christopher O'Malley, but there was nothing on record about either man. I was certain Riley had been the killer of the three people, plus possibly two others. The other person I suspected of being his contact, Paul Farrier, had been found dead in his car in Malmesbury. No one had been arrested for this and the reason for his being there had never been known.

Could it be Gavin whom Gant had asked for information about me? Working for an organisation like *Prevental*, he would certainly know about the movements of mercenaries and hitmen in and out the country. What would Gavin be doing involved in this?

"Unlikely, I'd have thought, though I'm not discounting it."

"He was never directly connected to that other case, was he?"

"No. I saw him with Farrier a couple of times but I couldn't ascertain whether he was an active participant in the deaths. I've an open mind on that, though."

"You may have to talk to him again."

"Could be," I replied.

"I heard, just before you came into the office, that MI5 had been to see Gant at his hotel this morning after your conversation with DI Harrow. He admits he and you talked for a while but he denied being the shooter in this case. Said he was back in the hotel before midnight, and CCTV suggests he was. He also claims that he was with a friend just beforehand, and this person can alibi him, so that seems to rule him out. When were the Phipps shot?"

"Around eleven thirtyish. Where's Gant staying?"

"Hotel on Park Lane."

"Plenty of time to get back, even if he walked."

"I'm waiting to hear if MI5 know why Gant's in the country. People like him aren't tourists. If he's in the country it's usually bad news for someone."

"Tell that to the mother of Paulie and Louis Phipps."

"Yes, well, other than that he's in the country, we haven't got anything on him. We can't hold him. We've only the Phipps' word he'd been shooting at them and their word wouldn't be reliable even if they were still with us."

"Are MI5 tailing him?" I asked.

"Wouldn't have thought so but there's no reason not to. He's entitled to go about his business until he steps out of line, then he'll be picked up and bundled out on the first plane."

I thought for a few moments. Looking out at the view of the park from the seventh floor always helped me concentrate better.

"We need to find out why Gant's in the country," I stated.

"How you going to do that, ask him nicely perhaps? "

Flippancy from Smitherman?

"Not just yet. I'm going to do some digging around. Someone must know him. Also, I'm going to check out the Phipps brothers, see what they've been up to. Maybe there's a link there."

"Until we're told otherwise, this is a straightforward murder case which CID will handle. We're not involved. What about the rest of your holiday?"

"Yeah, what about it?" I flashed him a knowing look.

I went to my desk. Actually it was the first desk available. I wasn't aware if the term 'hotdesking' was still part of current management-speak but, whatever, nobody had their own assigned desk any longer. Wherever there was a space was where you planted yourself.

I powered up my laptop and entered my password and code. I logged onto the Branch site that kept details of anyone known to the security services and entered the names Louis and Paulie Phipps. I drew a blank. Whatever nefarious misdeeds they'd committed were deemed unworthy of entry onto Special Branch records. I then went onto the Police National Computer and hit the jackpot.

Louis Phipps had been in and out of trouble his whole life. He had convictions in the Juvenile Court for theft, criminal damage and taking and driving away of motor vehicles and convictions in the Magistrates' Court for assault and being in possession of a small amount of marijuana. Paulie Phipps had only two convictions as he was with Louis when he'd stolen a car and also when Louis had been caught shoplifting in a West End branch of WH Smith, trying to steal a packet of coloured pens and a magazine. What a pair. The Phipps brothers were to virtue and integrity what a dog was to a tree.

I was puzzled. This was all penny ante stuff, the things punk kids do as teenagers before either they grow up, mature and leave trouble behind them or, in the case of people like Louis Phipps, use them as stepping stones to more serious, more organised criminal activity. Someone like Louis would probably have remained a punk forever had he not been killed.

Either way I could see nothing whatever on their records indicating even the smallest reason why a killer like Phil Gant would be on their tail. Most of his known associates were people of a similar ilk: losers, wasters and other lowlifes destined for a long stretch in a prison cell or the grave before their mid-twenties. On what I'd seen Gant wouldn't even look in their general direction, yet someone was paying him a lot of money to remove these two slimeballs from the planet. Why? I needed someone who knew Gant and would be prepared to talk about him.

Which is how, later that same morning, I came to be sitting opposite Richard Rhodes in a café off the Tottenham Court Road. I'd phoned a journalist I knew, Richard Clements. He was someone I'd known when I'd been a student at King's, London. We hadn't been friends; in fact I'd thought he was some left-wing lunatic spouting the usual clichés and mouthing the correct platitudes about all the 'right-on' causes the good radical supposedly believed in. But I'd come into contact with him again last year when looking into a murder case. We'd struck up some kind of almost mutual interest and I'd fed him pertinent information concerning that case, which I knew he would take to other journalists who had the right kind of connections and sources in the secret world, and this had led to journalists in the mainstream press taking a closer look at the case. When they decided to publish the results of their investigations, lawyers for the Government had gone to the High Court seeking an injunction, but this had been refused and *The Observer* published its story about the case and its suspicions that some kind of cover-up had occurred, which was why the full report was never published.

Clements himself still worked for the *New Focus*, a fortnightly left-wing publication for the intellectual leftie, and his standing in the profession had risen as a result of the leads he was able to give to senior writers who had contacts with MI5, which led to the High Court hearing. Clements said he didn't know any mercenaries or hired killers, and none of the crime correspondents he knew would have access to that kind of information.

However, he knew an ex-journalist, a man in his mid-sixties named Jerry, who used to be a war correspondent who'd covered conflicts all over the world and had extensive knowledge of and contacts in the world of the mercenary soldier. He'd given me the contact details and I'd visited the man at his flat by Regent's Park. He readily agreed to talk and, through this, I had details for Richard Rhodes, whom the writer was convinced knew Gant as they'd worked together in the Middle East. He'd interviewed Rhodes once because he was writing an article about mercenaries for the *Sunday Times* and used what he'd said as background. Jerry had contact details for Rhodes on his mobile, called him and told him who I was and what I wanted to talk to him about, though I wasn't too specific, and Rhodes agreed to meet in a café he knew near to Goodge Street Tube station, behind the Tottenham Court Road.

Richard Rhodes was an ex-marine who, after his time in the service of Queen and Country was up, had enlisted to fight as a mercenary in Southern Africa and, since then, in other theatres of war on more than one continent.

Actually, his time in the army had been curtailed rather suddenly as he'd fought a sergeant in his regiment who was widely regarded as a thug and a bully. Rhodes had refused to obey the orders of the sergeant when he'd given him a menial and humiliating task to do. A fight broke out and, after a bloody and epic brawl, Rhodes beat the sergeant into submission, and the sergeant would carry the scars from that brawl to his grave.

Rhodes was given the choice of resigning from the army with immediate effect or face a court martial and very likely a dishonourable discharge. As his contract was near to being completed, he chose to resign. Since then he'd become a soldier of fortune.

I pulled his security file before meeting him. He was a man who liked to fight, with or without weapons, in armed conflict or on the streets. He was completely amoral and would fight anyone for any reason. This had led to recent accusations of being involved in killing women and children, something he had strenuously denied when interviewed by an MI6 officer. He'd been arriving back in the UK from a tour of duty in the Lebanon and MI6 had taken him to one side and grilled him about his involvement in recent deaths in that country after complaints from the Lebanese Government about the involvement of foreign nationals in Beirut. Rhodes admitted involvement in the fighting but not in any action that had led to the deaths of women and children. No action was taken against him.

Currently between wars, the most recent intel available suggested he was working as a bodyguard for a Colombian who was suspected of being something high up in one of the main drug cartels that bedevilled that country but, on this day, when contacted by Jerry, his services had not been required so he agreed to meet up for a drink and a chat, especially when told it concerned his friend Gant, though I didn't spell out exactly why.

I was waiting in the café when he arrived. Even if I'd not seen his picture, I'd have known it was him the second he entered. He looked combative and physically imposing. He stood six foot two, weighed about sixteen stone and carried himself with all the nonchalance of someone who was sure he could put you on the ground if he had to. Only the crazy brave or the desperately suicidal would want to take him on in a one-to-one fight. Mickey was a skilled fighting man but I doubted even he could go up against Rhodes with any realistic chance of success.

He was wearing a combat jacket, black jeans, army issue boots and a black beret. His face was weather-beaten from the time spent in sunnier climes and he exuded an aura of 'do not mess with' as he moved. He looked at me and I nodded. He sat at my table. The young waitress took our tea and coffee order and went away. He reached out and we shook hands. His right hand was the size of a small shovel and, even with minimal force, he almost broke two of my fingers.

"So, why does Special Branch want to talk to me?" he

asked after saying how cold it was for the time of year and how he couldn't wait to get back to somewhere warmer after his work in London was up. His voice was raspy, as though he was still suffering the after effects of flu. The waitress brought our drinks.

"Your friend Gant," I replied.

"Why should I talk to you about him? What makes you think I even know him?"

"You agreed to meet up when I suggested it. Look, let's not insult each other's intelligence, eh? We both know you and Phil Gant are friends. I know for a fact you worked together on a hit in the Lebanon and, on your return to this country, MI6 grilled you about it at Heathrow, which means you'll probably be closely watched and monitored every time you come and go. I simply want to know what he's currently up to. I'm not looking to arrest you, I just want to talk. This simply has a bearing on a case I'm involved in. I'll file it as background. Gant doesn't have to know about it."

Rhodes took a bite of his biscuit and a sip of coffee whilst he thought about how much he wanted to tell me.

"Yeah, okay, Gant and I know each other," he said, still sipping his coffee.

"He stays at your place in Shoreditch occasionally, doesn't he?"

"You know about that place?" He looked surprised.

"I'm in Special Branch. You really think I couldn't find your address?" I smiled.

"Yeah, I suppose so," he nodded.

"So, Mr Phil Gant. What's he currently up to?"

Rhodes leaned forward slightly, almost conspiratorially.

"The word on the street is he's been hired to go after a guy who's trying to blackmail someone prominent in the Government."

"What, the Government here?" My eyes opened wide at the news.

"No, in Uzbekistan," he snapped sarcastically. "Where do you think? Of course it's here."

"What do you mean by 'Prominent'? How high up are we talking?"

"What do you mean?"

"Are we talking someone in the Cabinet? A minister? Secretary of State? An Under-Secretary of State? Someone with his finger on the political pulse? That kind of prominent."

"That I don't know. I just heard it was someone prominent."

"So, what's the blackmail angle?"

"Don't know that either. I just heard Gant had been hired to do a job of work in this country involving someone high up."

A job of work which had cost two people their lives. He made it sound as though Gant was going to be doing some painting and decorating.

"The two people Gant was after were a pair of losers, street punks who probably couldn't blow their own noses without someone directing it. I just don't see someone like Gant going after them. The idea of these two as part of some blackmail scheme . . ."

I let the sentence tail off.

"If Gant was hired, it's a safe bet whoever did it was certain of who he was after. Someone like Gant doesn't get hired mistakenly."

I thought for a moment. It still defied belief that a professional hitman like Gant was after two people like the Phipps brothers. Gant looking to eliminate someone who was supposedly trying to blackmail someone in, or close to, Government would make sense in his world. How could the Phippses be a part of this? They were both as thick as railroad spikes and yet they'd been killed by one of the world's best assassins. I was bemused.

"I'm also surprised Gant has been hired," he continued.

"Government has its own people to do this kind of work. Why bring in outsiders?"

"That would suggest this is some kind of private arrangement between whoever hired Gant and Gant himself. No official involvement, it would seem."

"Could be."

"How do you know all this?"

"Oh, come on, you know how it is. People know people, who talk to other people. In my world, it's known what's going on. Word gets around. You might not know exact details but you usually know the outline of what's happening."

"How did Gant get hired? He doesn't advertise in Yellow Pages and doesn't have a website that I know of, so if it's someone in Government circles, it's clearly someone with enough know-how to get in touch with the sordid world of the paid killer. Not everyone has that knowledge."

"Well, clearly whoever hired him does have, doesn't he?" He sat back in his chair taking in the surroundings, which were bland and mostly cheerless.

I thought for a moment.

"Let me tell you why I'm asking this."

Over the next few minutes I told Rhodes about the events of the previous evening, culminating with the two shots which killed the Phipps brothers. I reiterated my disbelief that someone like Gant could possibly be after punks like the Phippses and my astonishment that they could possibly have done anything to get a top-notch killer like Gant involved.

"A target's a target, irrespective," he said airily after I'd finished. "Doesn't matter whether they're punks or not. Someone wants them dead, they get removed. Come on, you're Special Branch; you know how people like Gant operate. They get contacted by a potential client who wants them to take out someone, and they agree or disagree. Gant wouldn't be concerned with the morality of it or whether they're just a pair of punk scumbags. He thinks the job's feasible, he takes it on if offered the right price. Same as I've done in his position."

"You've done jobs like this?"

"You'd be surprised at what I've done." He smirked. "But it wasn't in this country. My old granddad used to say you should never shit on your own doorstep." He laughed at his aphorism.

"So, how much is Gant getting paid for this heroic act?"

"No idea. Fees we don't discuss, but it's a fair bet it'd be worth his while," he said, grinning.

"When did you last see Gant?" I asked.

"Couple of nights back. Had a couple of beers with him. He gets in touch when he's in town, which isn't all that often now as I'm not always here either. But we keep in touch."

"He's staying at some hotel over Park Lane way, isn't he? Why isn't he staying at your place?"

Rhodes sipped his coffee.

"I'm away working a lot of the time. Also, I sometimes have others staying there, and it wouldn't be conducive for Gant to be there, given who these people are, you know?"

"Yeah, just imagine, Gant meeting up with a bunch of Colombians planning out wholesale distribution strategies for their cocaine imports. Can't have that now, can we?"

"You know what I'm currently doing?" He raised his eyebrows in surprise.

"Yeah, and who for. Really honourable work, isn't it, making it safe for some Colombian drug lord to put even more cocaine on the streets of London. Bit of a comedown after fighting in the Lebanon and wherever else you've been, isn't it?" I smiled at him sarcastically.

"Beggars can't be choosers, eh?" he replied airily. "Anyway, you know how much I get for this? Couple of grand a week, tax free, everything thrown in, plus I get to stay in their flash hotel over Knightsbridge way, and when it's finished, I'm promised a bonus."

He sounded as though he was bragging. I ignored it.

"So, according to you, if I heard you correct, there's no mistake here. Gant was definitely after the two he killed last night."

"Gant's only a suspect. You can't prove he killed them. It could just as easily be me who did it."

"Unlikely. Too good a shot for you. Whoever killed them took the shot in the dark and from quite a distance. That's top quality marksmanship. I doubt you qualify."

From the subtle shift in his posture, his body language told me he'd not been impressed with my last comment. I sipped my tea.

"You gonna arrest him, then?"

"I suspect I won't get close enough. Anyone as well connected as he seems to be will be seen by MI5 rather than me. Besides, arrest him for what? I didn't see anyone pulling a trigger. All we have is two dead bodies but no official suspects, and I suspect he'll be alibied up to his ears at the time of the deaths, so we're effectively screwed for the moment. Besides, given who the victims were, the Branch hasn't been called in. It's being treated as an ordinary murder by CID. Unless we can get evidence pointing the finger at Gant, we probably won't be either."

"In Gant's world, people who hire him tend to be quite high up and very well connected, if you know what I'm saying. Some of the kills he's carried out have been at the behest of people right at the heart of power, quite prepared to pay him a lot to eliminate someone," Rhodes stated.

"Enemies of the state are one thing but, as I said earlier, I don't see where the Phipps brothers fit into this moral equation."

"The only morality in the world Gant and I work in is paying someone on time after they've done what they were contracted to do," he said whilst smiling. "Someone deserves to die, they get removed. That's how it works."

"And who decides that one? Who makes him the moral arbiter of life and death?"

"The employee. An offer's made," he shrugged, "you decide whether it's worth doing or not. It's black and white really. I don't concern myself with other considerations."

It dawned on me to ask whether that included situations similar to the one in the Lebanon last year when twenty women and children had died in a gun battle between Government forces and rebel fighters, but there was nothing to be gained from debating morality with someone like Richard Rhodes. He was comfortable in his own skin about what he and Gant did, and he probably thought ethics was a county north east of London. But at least he'd given me something to follow up on. He'd confirmed Gant had been after the Phipps brothers. I still wanted to know why.

I drained my tea and stood up.

"Thanks for your help, anyway." I left money on the table to cover the drinks.

"Yeah, see you around."

I hope not, I thought as I left the café.

Back in the office I decided it was essential to find out everything I could about Louis and Paulie Phipps. What had they been doing in the past few months? If, as Rhodes had said, Gant had been hired to take out someone who was part of a scheme to blackmail someone in Government circles, where did the Phipps' fit into this? I very much doubted either of the brothers knew how to blackmail anybody. Engaging in this would take skill and patience to carry out to a logical conclusion, and it required the kind of animal cunning and a degree of intelligence I suspected neither brother possessed. The likes of Louis Phipps would want instant gratification for their deeds, and I very much doubted that the long game, planning and executing a blackmail scheme successfully, was part of his thought processes.

Besides, would you really use someone like Paulie Phipps in such a plan? He was too weak and stupid to tie his own shoelaces, so helping to plan a blackmail scheme was out of his league. I also doubted either of the brothers could even spell Government if their lives depended upon doing so.

No, I had to find out everything I could about the Phipps brothers. Perhaps doing that would enable me to ascertain the likely truth of Richard Rhodes' story about blackmail.

I already knew about their criminal records from the PNC. Neither Louis or Paulie Phipps were what could exactly be regarded as criminal masterminds. A conviction for trying to steal magazines and coloured pencils from WH Smith's? Hardly likely to challenge the Kray twins or the Chackarti family in criminal infamy. Most of the cases they'd been pulled for were non-contentious. The assault case had turned on the issue of self-defence, with Phipps claiming he was the victim in this case, but he'd been found guilty. Similarly the marijuana he'd been caught in possession of had been a minuscule amount and he'd been fined for possession. Apart from shoplifting and a few other minor scrapes with the law, there was little else to excite the imagination. But what caught my attention was the most recent conviction earlier this year for stealing a car.

They'd seen a car, a brand new Toyota Prius, parked up in a multi-storey car park near Waterloo station. Looking through the car window Louis Phipps had said he'd noticed two bags, a leather official-looking briefcase and a woman's shoulder bag. They'd broken the window, opened the door and started the car. They drove away and dumped the car by Herne Hill station, but kept the bags. So far, so typical.

But at this stage details became hazy. The car had been recovered and returned to the lawful owner but whoever that was had not been identified in the official report. The Phipps had been identified as the culprits, both from CCTV images and from fingerprints found on the steering wheel. They'd been prosecuted, found guilty and each drew a suspended sentence, with the magistrates saying that next time they would not be treated so leniently. It seemed the car owner was just pleased to have the car back and had decided that retribution was uncalled for, so had played no further part in the case.

Reading the transcript it occurred to me that nothing about either bag had been mentioned. From the make of car and the description of the two bags, I'd have expected to see at least some mention of them and some reference to the fact that neither had ever been recovered. Usually, the fact of property being stolen and unrecovered upon arrest was a factor in the sentencing process but that didn't appear to have occurred here.

The details from the hearing were sketchy. The case gave all the indications of having been dealt with somewhat perfunctorily and the brothers had left court as free men after drawing suspended sentences. Reading about it, I formed the impression that the case had been disposed of with an almost obscene haste.

I couldn't explain why but this case didn't feel right. Trials usually involved transcripts and details of occurrences, lost property and other relevant information but that wasn't the position here. The files gave more detail about stealing coloured pencils from Smith's than about the theft of a valuable car and its contents. Given that this was not exactly a first appearance before a court of law, I'd have expected to see more details. I read down the page but was none the wiser when I finished.

The arresting officer in the case had been a Detective Mullins, based at West End Central, which was where I'd been initially based after completing basic training at Hendon Police College. Mullins was someone I was aware of as he was stationed there when I'd first arrived, though we became professional colleagues rather than friends. I phoned the station. He was at his desk and he agreed to talk if I came to the station. So I did.

He shared a congested office with a number of others of

similar rank and below. The office was alive with activity; people were talking on the phone, shouting across the room to each other and typing on their laptops. Two officers nearby were attempting to talk to someone who, it seemed, was a reluctant witness to some criminal act, and trying to get him to embellish his story so it would stand up in court.

"Remember this?" Mullins said, waving his hand around the room. "It's called police work. You used to do it before you started chasing shadows. Remember that?"

I grinned at him, told him to fuck off and poured a coffee from the pot nearby. I moved a pile of files from a chair and sat at the desk opposite him. We made small talk for a few minutes, about who'd been promoted, who was in line for promotion after kissing the right arses at the right time, cases where they'd nicked someone they'd been after for quite a while, and his apprehension about a forthcoming trial where he was convinced some left-leaning, *Guardian*-reading, human-rights quoting barrister would get the accused off on a technicality.

"So, how can I help the Branch out?" he asked. "Is this about that case you were involved in last night where those two blokes got shot dead?"

"Yeah, it is; grapevine works fast round here, doesn't it? I wasn't actually involved in it. I just happened to be standing nearby when they'd got shot."

"How near?"

"Next to them."

Over the next few minutes I gave some details about the case, and ended by describing the deaths of the Phipps brothers. For the moment I omitted any reference to Gant and my belief, my certainty, that his was the gun that killed the Phippses.

"Louis Phipps's a real piece of shit. I've come across him a few times. A real pilgrim. I interviewed him after his drugs arrest and he's a nine carat turd. No surprise he's on the receiving end of a bullet. Someone like him was always likely to wind up dead sooner or later. It's not a Branch case, though, is it?"

"Not for the moment, no. It's being handled as a straightforward murder. The thing is," I kept my voice down even though it was noisy in the office, "I've had a whisper from someone that the Phippses were targeted because they were part of a conspiracy to blackmail someone and that's what got them killed."

Mullins looked aghast at that comment.

"Blackmail? Nah, not Louis's style at all." He shook his head in disbelief. "Someone like him doesn't do things like that. He'd be more likely to bang you over the head from behind and steal your wallet. Where'd you hear that?"

"Rather not say for the moment. I'm looking into his movements over the past few months. I've checked his record. It shows what he's been done for. The only thing he's done recently that got my attention, though, was being arrested and convicted for car theft."

"What about it? It isn't the first time that slimeball's nicked a car. There was no problem with it. Car was reported missing from where it had been parked and later found abandoned. It was dusted and we found Phipps' dabs all over the wheel. Got him easy as shooting goldfish in a bowl."

"Yeah, I know all that. Fingerprinting isn't routine in car thefts, though, is it?" I wondered. When I'd been a beat copper, any car we found that had been stolen was rarely fingerprinted, unless there was a suspicion it had been stolen to order, like a luxury sports car for instance.

"That's true, but we were asked to do it, so that's what we did."

"Who asked you?"

"DCI Tomkinson."

"A DCI? Really?"

"Yup. He was in charge of the investigation."

"Interesting. It's just a car theft. Why involve a DCI?

Another thing I don't get is the lack of any substantive detail in the report."

"What do you mean?" He sat back in his chair.

"Nothing about who the car belonged to or any reference to the bags that were taken, which it seems were never recovered. Things like that usually get included, yet they've been left out here. I was wondering why. Who did the car belong to?"

"I don't know. As I said, car was reported missing, suspected of being stolen. The plate numbers were circulated and we were asked to keep an eye out. Pair of uniforms in a car found it parked a couple of days later down Herne Hill way, dumped by Brockwell Park. They call it in and, after fingerprinting, Phipps was identified, arrested and charged. Easy peasy, mate."

"I don't get why he didn't go down either. He's got a record long as your left arm yet he gets a suspended sentence. Doesn't add up, does it?"

"Probably doesn't, but when does it ever? But at least we added another notch to his belt and he'd have gone down next time, except someone beat us to it." He said this in a deadpan manner.

I thought about what I'd heard for a few moments. I decided to raise the stakes.

"Off the record, strictly between you and me, was there any pressure put on you from above," my eyes looked upwards, "to close this case quickly, you know, wrap it up with the minimum of fuss? You know the kind of thing, don't probe too deeply, just get it done, something like that?"

"What are you saying?" His eyes narrowed.

"I'm not sure. The whole feel of this case is that it was dealt with as quick as possible. Who reported the car stolen? Things like that. None of this ever made it into any court report."

Mullins shifted slightly in his seat. The questions seemed

to make him uncomfortable. I couldn't work out why that was. He stood up.

"You want another tea or coffee?"

Before I could say no, he insisted I did and said we should get one downstairs. I followed him to the small canteen in the basement. It was still as tacky and in need of a fresh coat of paint as I remembered. He bought two cups of something that bore a passing resemblance to coffee, though not the actual taste, and we sat down. The Formica-covered tabletop told a story of many a stain from spilled drinks and cigarette burns, plus a few graphic designs etched from the edges of cutlery.

"This is off the record, Rob, you got that? You never heard this from me. Okay?"

I nodded my assent.

"The car was registered to a woman named Debbie Frost. It was her who reported it missing. Seemed quite frantic to get it back, she did. She also said there were a couple of items in the car, her bag and a briefcase belonging to someone she said she knew. We found the car but not the bags. The thing is," he leaned forward and lowered his voice, even though we were the only two people in the canteen, "the car was found a few days later where I said it was. She was contacted and told we'd got the car back but as of yet no bags recovered, but by then she said they weren't important and of no consequence so they didn't matter. Seemed strange 'cause, when she reported the car stolen, she was almost hysterical. Implied something about her boss being real pissed off if the bags were lost. Yet a few days later she's almost blasé about the whole thing. Says it doesn't matter about the bags, she was just pleased to get the car back as it was a new one and she'd not had it too long."

"Did she say who the other bag belonged to?"

"I don't think she did, no."

"Why she was parked up in Waterloo; she work in that area?"

"Don't know."

"How long had the car been there?"

"Not that long, couple of hours maybe."

"Was it just Phipps' prints on the steering wheel?"

"His and Debbie Frost's. Hers were all over the place."

"And I don't suppose she said what was in the missing bags?"

"Got it in one."

"Did she even give a statement? There doesn't appear to be any record of one being taken."

"No, I don't think she did. I certainly didn't take one from her. She reported the car missing but I'm not aware she gave a written statement to anyone."

I thought about what I'd heard for a couple of moments.

"What does all this suggest to you?"

"At this point, nothing. Most people aren't too worried about what was in their car; they just want the vehicle back. What *was* strange, though, was that the Phippses were initially brought in and questioned by me and another officer. During the interview, we get called to go see the boss, and the interrogation is continued by two other guys from Century House."

That could mean only one thing.

"MI5 questioned the Phippses?" I was surprised.

"So it would appear. Soon after they get taken out and questioned somewhere else and that's the last we hear until the case goes to the Magistrates' Court and they get their knuckles rapped."

Mullins drained his coffee and wiped his mouth with the back of his hand.

"So maybe your story about his trying to blackmail someone isn't as ridiculous as it seemed."

Richard Rhodes had said that Gant was hired because Phipps was trying to put the squeeze on someone in Government circles. That suggested Phipps knew something about someone that that person would rather not have made known. Is that why Gant had been hired, to silence Phipps before he could disseminate whatever it was he'd learned from his theft? What could he have learned that someone was prepared to pay top dollar to an assassin like Gant to cover up? I was still in the dark.

"I think whatever's in that case is what got those two killed. Something doesn't add up here. Why involve MI5 in a car theft?"

"There's no suspects so far, is there?" This was stated rather than asked.

"Nope. I've given a statement to a DI Harrow, so has Mickey. It was outside his bar the shootings occurred. There was nobody in the street so we're the only witnesses to what happened. I've no doubt this will remain as an unsolved murder unless CID gets a break."

Mullins looked at me for a few moments. He was weighing up everything said so far and putting his own slant on it. He nodded then grinned almost quizzically.

"That's not what you think, is it? You know more than you're letting on, don't you?"

"Not sure," I mused, "but I'll be sure to keep you out of it whatever turns up."

After a little more small talk about the failure of our respective teams to set the Premiership on fire this season, I thanked Mullins for his time and left to return to the Yard. My earlier suspicion about the case not being quite kosher had been mildly vindicated.

I went on the PNC again. I was re-covering earlier ground, looking at the files on Louis Phipps and his brother. Louis had been born in Naples but had moved to London with his family when he was one year old. Paulie had been born in London. The family name was Phipperanio but the father had Anglicised it soon after coming to this country.

The files gave details of scholastic achievements, which meant permanent exclusion at fifteen for Louis and Paulie leaving at sixteen before taking GCSEs. Their employment history showed they'd rarely kept any paid employ for long, with Louis often being sacked for insubordination.

Louis Phipps now had six court appearances to his name, with offences ranging from possession of a controlled substance and assault to the most recent, which was car theft. He'd never done time in prison, the nearest being an overnight remand when arrested for assault occasioning ABH whilst waiting to be arraigned. Paulie had never seen the inside of a cell either and I'd no doubt that, but for what happened last night, they'd not last too much longer on the street.

I could sum up the life histories in their files as the chronicles of a pair of losers. In fact, had they been able to write their combined autobiographies, this would have been a good working title. It all made their alleged graduation to attempting to blackmail someone in Government somewhat hard to swallow.

I was still thinking about what I'd read when a voice disturbed my reverie.

"For someone on holiday, you're in here a lot today."

It was Smitherman.

"What are you doing? Aren't you supposed to be catching up on your reading? That's what you told me last week you were going to be doing."

"Change of plans. That was before some gunman shoots the Phipps brothers in front of me and seems to be going to get away with it."

Smitherman sat down by the side of the desk.

"If you're alluding to Gant, I told you he was interviewed by MI5 early and his story that he was in his hotel checks with hotel CCTV. He was definitely there around midnight. He was seen in the hotel lobby talking to someone. There were no witnesses to the shooting other than you and your pal, Corsley, and you've both been eliminated from police enquiries as your gun hadn't been fired, neither had the one Corsley had behind the bar. Both the Phippses' guns hadn't been fired either so, unless someone comes in and confesses, we're stuck. We'll keep the file open, of course, and CID are out and about talking to anyone who was known to Phipps to see if we can get a line on what he'd been up to, but I have to say the longer this investigation stretches out, the less optimism I have of a win."

"I've been looking into this case. Well, not this actual case. I've been checking out Louis Phipps and his brother, trying to see what they could have gotten into to get someone to set Gant after them."

"You're convinced it was Gant, aren't you?"

"What do you think? I see the guy outside the bar and he admits he's after the Phippses. They leave the bar, they get shot by someone who's clearly an expert marksman; two shots fired, one in the heart and one between the eyes. Both killed by someone with a trained eye. Gant, a top-notch killer, just happens to be nearby, and he also just happens to be a Special Forces trained marksman. He's also a known assassin. Kills to order. Coincidence? I don't buy it."

"It's not a Branch matter just yet, Robert, so we can't just go steaming in. It's difficult to imagine any real security issues arising from killing the Phippses. Don't get me wrong, I don't want unsolved murders around here any more than anyone else does, but we have to be circumspect about it. CID is investigating this matter. Let them handle it. Go back to your holiday, Rob."

He stood up. He gathered his papers and left the room. His recommendation I continue with my holiday was only a suggestion but, in his eyes, it had the force of a direct order. In circumstances like this there was only one thing to do to alleviate my frustration. Before catching the Tube home I stopped at the pub opposite St James's Park station and had a few beers. Works every time. I felt better and continued reading my book well into the night.

Whilst in the pub I saw a newspaper. The *London Evening Standard* led with the murders of two unnamed men the previous evening. The story said they'd been leaving a pub in Bayswater at closing time when a person or persons unknown ambushed them and shot both men dead. Happily there were no pictures of the crime scene or the bodies, though there was a picture of the street taken from the Kensington Gardens end. The paper carried brief details of the victims, which did not make either man sound like a candidate for sainthood in whatever church they worshipped, hinting at all manner of misdemeanours and brushes with the forces of Law and Order. Nothing was mentioned about the holding of hostages in the bar and it mentioned the police at the moment having no solid leads as to who the killer might be. I certainly knew who it was though I could not prove anything. I wondered if this was how their mother found out about the fate of her sons.

THREE
Wednesday

THE DAY BEFORE, looking through the PNC files on Louis Phipps, I'd made a note of his address and any known associates. A motley crowd indeed, the majority having had some contact with law enforcement during their upbringing, usually an arrest and court appearance, though none had committed what could be perceived as serious crime. They were all just like Phipps – killing time until they finally started lengthy prison sentences for having been dumb enough to have dreams of avarice but neither the means nor the brains to make them come true, or, as was the case with Louis and Paulie, avoid an early grave. The majority of the Phippses' friends were late teens to early twenties and sensing their likely fate was depressing.

As this wasn't technically a case I was directly involved in, and certainly not a Special Branch one yet, Mickey agreed to come along and keep me company. The presence of two police officers usually suggested to the likes of Phipps' boon companions that they meant business, just like when the bailiffs arrive.

The brothers had lived in Brixton so we started there. I parked on the main road near to where the Phippses lived, on a road close to the Loughborough estate, not too far from the centre of Brixton. They were hard-to-let houses previously under local authority control but now run by a Housing Association. Their house was on Barrington Road and we soon found the number we were looking for. Walking along we were subjected to some threatening glances and suspicious stares from the mainly black youths who were either leaning against walls or just walking around giving a successful impression of having nothing to do and nowhere to do it. From the glares we elicited it was clear they knew we were police. There was a solitary black male, probably late twenties, standing on the corner constantly looking around. He looked across the road at us, looked to his left and shook his head slightly. Immediately a car started up and pulled away from the kerb.

"What do you reckon, the lookout for street sales?" Mickey grinned.

I shrugged.

At Phipps' house I rang the doorbell. Ten seconds later I rang it again. I heard the muffled sounds of someone shuffling down the corridor. The door opened and I saw a teenage girl, maybe sixteen, wearing a white baggy T-shirt with a faded print of Miss Piggy on the front and a pair of multi-coloured shorts. I wasn't actually certain if the shirt was white as there were so many stains and it was faded in places. She wore nothing on her feet, which were very dirty.

"Yeah, what you two want?" Her accent was coarse and she sounded raspy.

"Always spot class, can't you?" I heard Mickey whisper.

"What you just say?" she said loudly.

"He didn't say anything," I said as I showed her my ID card. "I'm DS McGraw, this is my colleague, Mr Corsley. I believe this is where Louis Phipps lives." I tried to sound authoritative.

"What if he does? He ain't here if you're looking for him, ain't been here for a few nights and I don't know where he is either."

"That's true, and he may not be coming back tonight either as he's somewhat indisposed," Mickey said with a straight face. "We need to look at his flat."

"Why? What you wanna snoop around there for?"

She was truly obnoxious, this kid. Just as well she wasn't bright enough to ask if we had a search warrant. As she spoke a man walked along the corridor. He was around six foot and pencil thin. He had a wispy beard and dreadlocks reaching his chest. It was hard establishing if he was black or white as his skin was the colour of parchment. From the brownish hair colour I guessed white. Up close his eyes betrayed the fact he was a junkie. They were bloodshot and unfocused, with dilated pupils, and his face had the kind of acne that would have a teenage girl thinking about suicide.

"Can I be of assistance, Officers?" He smirked. His voice sounded as if he had a throat infection.

I identified myself again and repeated that I needed to look at Louis Phipps' flat. He too didn't mention asking to see a warrant. They didn't seem to breed them too bright down this way.

"Flat's on the top floor, man, but, like, I don't have the key."

"That's no problem. Like, I have one, man," Mickey replied facetiously. The man hadn't spotted Mickey spoofing him or, if he did, he ignored it. Maybe he'd not understood it.

"Okay, come in."

The man stepped aside and we entered.

"There's only one flat up there, it's easy to find," the man called out as we ascended the stairs.

The two flights of stairs were an ordeal. Not in terms of height, in terms of hygiene. The whole place stank. There was a foul odour of sweat and unwashed bodies. There were cobwebs across the corners of the stairs and there were several tears in the wallpaper. The window on the first floor was covered in grime, making it difficult to see through. Graffiti covered one wall and someone had attempted a mural on the wall opposite. The floor was thick with dust, sufficient to leave a footprint. The place was a slum.

We reached the second floor. There was only one door.

"You got the key. Open it," I said.

Mickey nodded. He turned to his left, leapt forward and, with his right foot, kicked the door on the handle. It crashed open against the wall. The wood around the lock was rotted and we could have probably opened the door by sneezing against it.

"This is technically illegal, isn't it?" Mickey asked.

"Very illegal," I agreed. We entered the flat. There was a short corridor leading into a main living room. There was a small bathroom and toilet off to the left. There was a kitchen next to the toilet and, further into the room, another door which led into a bedroom. The main room was around twenty feet square with a window opposite the kitchen door. In the corner of the room was a large flatscreen television set that looked brand new and top of the range. I wondered where Phipps had stolen it from.

The flat was the mess I'd expected. There were empty beer cans on the kitchen table and piles of discarded fast food wrappers in a bin filled to overflowing. There was sufficient dust on the floor to qualify to be topsoil. The whole flat had a pervasive sense of gloom. I looked out the window in the front room. I could see the street but only just as it was as grimy as the window on the stairs. There were brown stains on the ceiling, suggesting that the room had seen a considerable amount of smoking over time.

"Let's just do this and get the fuck out," Mickey said. I agreed.

I searched the front room. I looked in all the cupboards, under the settee and everywhere that looked like it could store something. There was a wardrobe with a few jackets and shirts hanging up and I searched all the pockets but found only lint. There was a pile of DVDs on the shelf and the majority were pornographic. I opened a few cases to see what else might be there but found nothing except the actual DVD. I found a mug on the kitchen table that had enough mould on the bottom to justify calling it penicillin.

I wasn't even sure what I was looking for. I was hoping to find something that stood out, something that someone like

Louis Phipps wouldn't usually be associated with but, whatever it was, I didn't find it. All we found was a tip.

Mickey had searched the bedroom. Under the beds there were piles of rubbish that had been simply swept out of sight. There was lots of dirty laundry and a couple of porno mags. The room was in the same state of squalor as the rest of the flat. Mickey looked through the bed sheets but there was nothing. The sheets were discoloured and looked like they'd not seen detergent for a very long time and, from the stains on them, whoever slept in this bed either had sex regularly or jerked off into the sheets. My money was on the latter.

I looked in the bathroom, which was as unhygienic as any I'd ever seen. There was the tang of someone having thrown up recently and the sour smell not successfully dissipating. At least the toilet had been flushed but the bowl was a colour I didn't recognise as hygienic. The cabinet contained just razors, some deodorant and a bottle of mouthwash. A couple of cockroaches scurried away under a crack in the pelmet.

After twenty minutes the only thing we had to show for our efforts was nausea. Mickey opened the fridge and saw a few cans of beer. He took one and opened it.

"I don't think he'll miss this. Cheers, Louis," he toasted him and drank. The fridge contained several food items that, from the rancid smell, had easily exceeded their use-before date. I closed the fridge.

Mickey drained the beer can, scrunched it up and tossed it on top of an already full wastepaper basket.

I was dispirited. I'd been hoping to find something I could tie to Phipps and the idea he'd been involved in a blackmail scheme but nothing here suggested anything other than someone for whom housework was anathema. If cleanliness was indeed next to Godliness, the Phipps brothers were practising heathens.

*

We went back downstairs. There was music coming from the kitchen so we headed there. The man was sitting at the kitchen table alongside the girl. The kitchen didn't look much tidier than the rest of the house but at least the surfaces looked cleaner and the only aroma came from something cooked earlier. Mickey stood by the cooker looking at right angles to the man leaning back in the chair. The girl eyed him suspiciously but said nothing. I saw a chair and sat down.

"Find anything?" He grinned. His teeth were discoloured and at least two from the top row were missing. I hoped he didn't like eating crunchy apples.

"No, nothing. I'd like to ask you a few questions, if you don't mind."

"Sure thing." He smiled at us.

"First off, who are you two and what's your connection to this place?"

"I live here. Name's Rudolf, this is Twinky." He nodded at the girl.

"Nice name," Mickey said. She glared at him as though wanting to say something but didn't.

"How long have Louis and Paulie Phipps lived here?"

"Middle of last year, I think." He paused. "Yeah, about a year sounds right."

"What does he do? You know, do either of them have paid employ?"

"Leave it out, man." Rudolf appeared to be choking back a laugh. "They're a pair of scallywags, ducking and diving, a bit of this, bit of that, you know what people like them are like."

"How did they pay their rent?"

"In cash, usually at the end of the month after I'd remind Louis it was due."

"I'm guessing they were successful duckers and divers. I mean, how else could they afford to live in the penthouse suite here?" I looked upwards.

I was purposely trying to antagonise Rudolf. I didn't like him. I didn't like his appearance; his telephone wire hair or his scruffy attire and his blasé indifference to the world around him. I didn't like the fact he was a junkie, probably permanently stoned. He sensed my resentment and shuffled slightly in his seat.

"Don't be so hostile, man. I'm answering your questions, aren't I? What you want to know?"

"Tell me what dear old Louis has been up to for the past few months. What's been his main source of income?" I said neutrally.

"Mainly drug dealing. He buys and sells, mainly marijuana and a bit of cocaine. He sometimes sells ecstasy as well."

"Sweet Mary Jane," Mickey said to no one in particular.

"Who does he buy from and who does he sell it on to?"

"Oh, come on, man, you know how many people around here use that stuff? Selling stuff round here is easy, man. Everyone wants it."

"What else does he do?"

"He likes mugging students," Twinky volunteered. "There's lots living round this way. Louis and his brother swipe their money and their mobiles and sell them on."

"I believe his recent misdemeanours also include carjacking." I stated flatly.

"Oh yeah man, yeah, he did. Real excited about that one. Said it was going to make him rich."

"Rich? What did he mean?"

"He didn't actually say what or how. It was Paulie who said the car they filched had something valuable the owner would want back and would pay a good price for it."

I was very interested in this.

"Okay, from the beginning. Tell me everything Phipps said about this. It's very important you leave nothing out. I need to know exactly what he meant." I said this slowly and firmly.

"Didn't really say that much, just said they'd ripped off a motor by Waterloo station and there were a couple of bags in the car. One was a briefcase and Phipps said what was in it would make him rich. I didn't really believe him. Phipps was always talking about some deal, some scheme or other that would make him a shitpile of money; none of them ever came off so I didn't take too much notice of this one either. Anyway, he gets busted a few days later as he'd dumped it by Brockwell Park." He smiled. "Just after that, police came and searched the flat."

"The police searched his flat?"

"Yeah."

"They take anything?"

"It was just one guy. I saw him leave. He didn't have anything I could see."

The Phipps brothers had stolen a car. Why search their home as a result?

"I didn't ask what he was looking for. Guy seemed real heavy, man. I was relieved after he left."

"Heavy, in what sense?" I was curious.

"Hard to say. I just got the impression he wasn't ordinary police. This guy had an aura, y'know? We've been searched a few times by Drugs Squad but this guy wasn't the same. He had, I don't know, an edge, something almost frightening. You could see it in his eyes, man. That dude was on a mission."

I looked at Mickey. He was leaning back against the cooker with his arms folded taking in everything he'd heard. I was trying to take it all in. What could Rudolf be referring to by saying this guy was heavy?

"Has this person, whoever he was, been back again?"

"No, man, he's not. I don't want him in this place again."

"Did you go up to the flat and see if he'd removed anything?"

"I just went upstairs, put the latch down on the door and shut it. I didn't go into the flat. Phipps doesn't like anyone in his place unless he invites them, you know what I'm saying? He can be a nasty son of a bitch, that Phipps."

"What happened when Phipps was released?" Mickey interjected.

"Nothing really, man. They just came back here and carried on. They went to court but just got a suspended sentence. Things just went along all tickety-boo until a little while ago."

"What happened?"

"They came back one night last week shitting themselves, especially the younger one," Twinky volunteered. She seemed to find this quite amusing and was smiling.

"Yeah," Rudolf agreed. "Apparently, someone told them they were going to kill them. Supposed to have taken a shot at them as they were on their way home. Scared the crap outa them, man. Whoever it was did it again a few nights back but, since then, neither of the Phipps have been here. Is that why they ain't been back lately, they in hiding?"

"Did they say who it was?" I ignored the question.

"Yeah, but I can't remember the name they gave." Rudolf looked apologetic.

This accorded with what Louis Phipps had said. It would suggest that Phipps had taken something from the car and someone had hired Gant either to retrieve it or, failing that, eliminate the person responsible for it being missing. Gant doesn't exactly work for a few pounds and a four-pack of beer so, if this was the case, whatever it was had to be something very important to someone.

I looked at Mickey as if to ask if he had anything else to ask. He shook his head. I stood up.

"Anyone living round here who Phipps sold drugs to, or was a friend and would know something about his recent movements?" I asked.

Rudolf looked at me as though I'd asked him to expose himself to his mother.

"Yeah, there's a few, man. Why's that?" He had some kind of bemused expression on his face.

61

"Why do you think, pigbreath? I wanna invite them to come dancing with us."

Mickey pushed himself upright from the cooker as he spoke. Rudolf shuddered in his seat.

"Just want to ask about Phipps. I won't use your name," I said.

Rudolf looked at Twinky almost pleadingly, as if she could impart any guidance or wisdom to him. She gave a non-committal shrug and went back to twirling the split-ends of her hair around her fingers.

"Okay, man, there's a cat named Simeon, lives at number 15, round the corner. They stayed there a coupla nights after the shooting thing. Don't tell him I mentioned his name."

I nodded. Mickey walked towards the front door. I followed.

"I'm serious, man, don't mention my name to Simeon. You said you'd not use my name. You promised, right?" He sounded scared.

"Promise? I just said I wouldn't use it. That's not a promise."

We left Rudolf feeling most aggrieved at his lot in life.

Number 15 was a short stroll away. The same guy we'd passed earlier was in the same position and his eyes followed us as we walked. As we drew parallel with him, he nodded and the next second a car started and drove away in the opposite direction. The area seemed to be populated with people either looking to buy or sell drugs of some kind.

We located Simeon's house. The front door was badly charred, almost as if someone had tried to burn it down. The letter box was bent out of shape and the button of the doorbell was hanging by a wire. There was a small front garden containing an overflowing waste bin and there were a considerable number of empty containers, wrappers and bottles surrounding it. I could hear music. Sounded like rap, a genre I particularly despised because of its racist and misogynistic overtones.

"Ol' Phippsy certainly knew the best addresses, eh?" Mickey said sarcastically.

I knocked on the front door. Twice. A man eventually answered. He stared blankly at us.

"What?" His tone was not inviting.

"DS McGraw, looking for Simeon." I flashed my ID card at him.

"He's kind of indisposed at present." The man smirked as he spoke.

"Is he in the house?"

"Oh yeah, man, he's in alright." He grinned.

"He's not indisposed, then, is he?"

I walked past the man and into the hallway, to be met by the all-pervasive aroma of marijuana. The smell was rich and intense. If we stood here long enough we could get stoned simply breathing.

"Which room?" I asked the man.

"He won't like you barging in." He raised his eyebrows.

"Do I really look like I give a fuck whether he'll like it or not?" I replied somewhat brusquely.

"No, you don't." He sounded annoyed. "Top of the stairs, first on the right."

I went up the stairs. Mickey followed. At the door I could hear a woman moaning in some kind of assumed ecstasy and there was a sound of bedsprings squeaking. We both laughed.

"It ain't gonna be your day, Sim," Mickey said. He rapped on the door.

"Fuck you want, man? Told you not to disturb me," a voice called out.

"Police. Open up," I said formally, trying not to laugh at Mickey's smirking.

The squeaking stopped. I could hear muffled voices and the sound of frantic scurrying around in the room. A few moments later the door opened and we were confronted by a black male, around mid to late twenties, hastily buttoning up a pair of jeans. He had the disturbed expression men frequently wore when experiencing coitus interruptus. He was bald, about six foot and rake thin. His ribs protruded to such an extent they resembled xylophones. He could be a poster boy for the after-effects of a starvation diet. I showed him my ID.

"Need to talk to you. Can we use your room?"

"Be easier to talk downstairs. My room's kind of occupied."

"I don't blush, honestly, and I promise not to look," Mickey said, not quite managing to keep a straight face.

Simeon looked as though he wanted to take a swing at Mickey, which would have been a big mistake on his part. He realised this and nodded.

"Let's go downstairs, eh?" I offered.

Simeon sat in an armchair and stared at us. We were in the front room and it wasn't an advert for the Ideal Home Exhibition. It was cold and smelled musty with mould and damp growing on the walls and there was something looking like dog shit lying on the floor in the corner. Simeon seemed oblivious, probably still thinking about what he was missing upstairs. He lit up a smoke.

"How'd you get onto me? Who told you about me?"

"Guy out there on the corner," Mickey said before I could say anything. "I asked if he knew someone called Simeon around this area and he directed us here."

"Yeah, but how did you actually get hold of my name?"

"Well, you know how it is, people talk about things and someone we talked to knew you and pointed us in your direction."

Simeon seemed satisfied with that explanation.

"So, what you wanna know?"

He slung a long leg over the arm of the chair and slouched down.

"You know Louis and Paulie Phipps, don't you?"

He nodded. "Yeah, 'course I do."

"How long you known Louis Phipps?"

"Since he moved down this way. Probably a few years or so."

"You close friends?"

"Me and Louis are tight, man." He raised his clenched left fist to make a point.

"Let's see, Phipps is a known drug seller but he has to get his stuff from somewhere. From the smell here I'm guessing it's you. You the candyman, Sim? You supplying for others to sell?"

He looked nervous. One moment he was in the throes of passion, the next he's being quizzed about his friends and selling drugs by police.

"Look, Sim, just answer a few questions as best you can and we'll forget how much dope there has to be here to be this pungent. Sound fair?"

He exhaled. "Alright," he muttered.

"Good. I wanna know what you know about Phipps' recent movements. You know, what's he been doing, where he's been hanging out, who with, things like that. Can you help us out?"

"Why should I?" He sounded petulant.

"Well, let's see," I mused. "I can see dog shit on the floor. What would the public health inspector make of that? And I do believe I can smell marijuana; let's bring Drugs Squad in. The woman who's upstairs. Go see if she's older than 16." Mickey grinned and stood up.

"Okay, okay, man."

He looked directly at us for the obligatory few seconds.

"Louis's into all kinds of bad shit, man. He sells dope, does the odd robbery, gets into the occasional fight. He's a piece of work, ol' Louis." He sounded almost proud.

"I know most of that. What I particularly want to know about is a car theft he did recently."

"He went to court for that. Got a suspended."

"Yes, but as well as stealing the car, there were two bags in the car and they seem to be unaccounted for. What do you know about that?"

Simeon started to look out the window. He nodded for a few moments and took a deep breath.

"I don't know anything about that," he finally replied.

"Really?"

"Yeah, really, man. I don't know anything about no bags. I know he boosted a car, but that's about it. Don't know anything else." He shook his head.

That he was lying was as obvious as the ribs sticking from his chest. He looked nervous, as if he was scared.

"Look, I'll level with you. Louis's in a little trouble just now about those bags."

This was true. I didn't mention the trouble had produced fatal consequences.

"So I need to know where they are or, if not, what was inside and what Phipps did with them."

Simeon pursed his lips and looked between Mickey and me. He sighed.

"Phipps said he'd stolen this flash new motor. He gave it to the guy who'd asked him to do it and, when he'd taken what he wanted, left the car. Louis dumps the car but gets nicked a bit later."

"Back up a moment. You say the car was stolen to order?"

"That's what it seemed to be from the way Phipps described it."

"Who asked him to do that? Who was Phipps doing this for?"

"Never said." Simeon shook his head. "Just said someone asked him if he wanted to earn some easy bread. All he had to do was to go to this car park near Waterloo and boost a motor and take it someplace. He does that but when the guy comes for it, he just took some stuff from a bag. Still paid him for his troubles. Phippsy dumps the car and got busted soon after."

‐‐‐‐‐‐ ◄◊► ‐‐‐‐‐‐

"He say why this guy wanted the car?"

"Nope. He didn't say why, at least not to me."

Curious.

"What did he say about the two bags?"

"One was a woman's handbag. Just had the usual shit women carry with them everywhere. The other one was a briefcase. Had lots of papers and apparently quite a number of photographs."

"Photographs?" I repeated.

"Yeah."

"Of who or what?"

"He didn't say; just said there were a number of files in the bag and, in one of the files, there were a lot of photographs."

"Did he say anything about the files, about what was in them, anything like that?"

"Not really. But he did say it was gonna make him and his brother rich."

"How?" Rudolf had said something similar just now.

"Never said. Just said the guy in the photos would pay a lot of bread to get them back. He said they were explosive."

"How did Phipps know that?"

"From the man who got him to boost the car. Said something about the bag containing something that would be very valuable."

What could Phipps have stumbled upon?

"Think back. What else did he say about the contents of the bag? Anything you can remember would be a big help."

"I can't think of much else, man."

"Was there anything in the handbag to indicate who it belonged to?"

"Yeah, and Phipps got in touch with her. Found a phone number in the bag. Said he'd talked to some woman on the phone but she told him he'd regret it if he didn't just give it all back."

"What, she threatened him?"

"Just swore loudly at him. I could hear it from where I was. She was no lady, man." He laughed.

"Did he ever meet this woman?"

"Never mentioned it if he did."

Fortunately I knew who she was.

"Were the bags in plain sight?" I asked.

"Huh?"

"Were the two bags clearly visible when he stole the car? You know, lying on the back seat out in the open where anyone could see them?"

"No. Louis said they were hidden under the front seat. Yeah, I remember now. Louis said the guy who wanted the car looked at one of the bags, took something out and put them back. He said he didn't want the car. Louis dumped the car but kept the bags. Thought there might be something worth his while in one of them, which is where he found the photos and the other shit in there."

"I don't suppose he told you what he did with them, did he?" I asked again, more in hope than expectation.

"No, man, he didn't."

"Could he have stored them somewhere?"

Simeon shrugged. "Dunno, might have done but I wouldn't know where."

I looked around the room. It looked no better on a second viewing. Simeon sounded like an educated man. Why would he choose to live like this? Mickey was standing, looking out the window at something I couldn't see.

"Why did he tell you all this? Surely if he'd stolen something this valuable, from the sound of it, he'd keep it to himself," I wondered out loud.

"He owed me money for some dope I supplied him with. A fucking lot of dope, man. He sold it all but I never saw the bread. He comes round here and says he's onto something that's gonna make him rich and, if I can wait a little while, he'll get me all I was owed, with more on top."

"And you believed him?"

"He was really excited about it. He was always talking shit about how he was gonna do this and that but he was high about this one, man. I sort of gave him a little time to get rich and pay me and I'm still waiting."

Just don't take a deep breath, I thought. From his expression, Mickey thought the same thing.

"Anything else you can tell me about Phipps and this mystery person who's going to make his dreams come true?"

"Not really, that's all I know about it."

"Did Phipps tell you someone took potshots at him and his brother recently?"

Rudolf seemed to know about this. What did Simeon know?

"Oh yeah, he did." Sim suddenly seemed more alive. "Came here a few nights back and asked if he could crash down here as someone had just fired at him and he didn't wanna go back to his place in case the guy knew where he lived. I asked what it was about and he said something about some American coming up to him in a pub and saying he was going to kill 'em both. Straight up, man, that's what he said." Simeon's voice was sounding slightly higher.

"Did he say why this guy said that?"

"No. Louis said he didn't believe it at first but, when this maniac appears across the street and takes a shot, he realised the guy meant it. In fact, come to think of it, I ain't seen Louis since he stayed here just before last weekend. He hiding someplace from this guy?"

"I've no idea where Phipps is right now."

This was true. I didn't know where his dead body had been taken.

"Guns. Trying to prise money out of people? What's Louis Phipps got himself into?

"I don't know, man, but this sounds like some heavy shit to me." Sim sounded concerned. "I think he's got a gun but it's mainly for show, y'know? Carries it around 'cause it reinforces his belief he's some big time dealer. I don't think he's ever used it."

"So, you don't know what Phipps stole from the car or why it was going to make him rich."

"I don't, man."

"Would you have any idea where he might have put the bags? If they're going to earn him a lot of money, presumably they'd have to be put somewhere safe. You know where?"

"You've already asked me that once. 'Fraid I don't. He never told me. He lives near here. You can look there if you want."

I was thinking we'd not get much else out of Simeon when the door opened and a girl wearing just a large baggy pyjama top entered. She was white, very thin and looked around 16. I hoped she was older. Even with the baggy top, it was obvious she was flat chested. Coupled with her cropped blonde hair, she looked androgynous. Her eyes suggested she'd been chemically stimulated earlier and was still coming down. Two skinny bodies like these in sexual congress would be almost combustible, like two pieces of kindling wood rubbing up to each other.

"Who you talkin' to, Sim? You coming back up?" She sat on the edge of the chair.

"Guys are police," he replied nodding towards us.

"Who are you?" I asked the girl.

"Name's Belinda."

"Beauty and the Beast," Mickey said. "Shouldn't you be at school?"

"I left school last year. I'm nearly 19. I'm a university student," she said matter-of-factly.

I wondered if she knew anything.

"Do you know a Louis Phipps?" I asked.

"That's your creepy friend, isn't it?" She looked at Simeon. "I know who he is but I don't know him. He's just someone used to come here once in a while but I tried not to be around when he did. His brother was cute but a bit of a wimp."

"So you don't know anything about him or what he's been up to."

"I'm sorry, no. What's he done this time?"

"Usual stuff. We're just following up a lead about him."

Mickey and I rose from our seats.

"Thanks for your time. Sorry we came at an, er, inappropriate time."

"Where do you go to college?" Mickey asked the girl.

"University of Greenwich. Simeon's my psychology tutor, aren't you, Sim?"

"Sure am, baby," he replied with a satisfied grin on his face, patting her naked thigh.

"You're a psychology lecturer and have a sideline selling drugs," Mickey stated flatly. "Does your Faculty Head know about your extra-curricular activities?"

"Hey, come on, man, I told you everything." Simeon looked very worried.

"You just keep this conversation to yourself and maybe he'll never know." I smiled. Simeon agreed that silence was indeed a virtue.

We thanked them for their cooperation and left. Walking back to the car I thought about what we'd heard from Rudolf and Simeon in the past hour.

"One-to-one tutoring has certainly changed since I left King's," I said as we got into the car.

In the last ninety minutes I'd learned that Louis Phipps believed he'd stumbled onto something that was going to make him rich. Both Rudolf and Simeon had said this. I'd also learned that Phipps had stolen the car after being paid to do so, but the instigator had not wanted the car after perusing the contents of the bags, whereupon it appeared Louis Phipps had helped himself to the two bags and, so far as I could tell, they'd not materialised. Phipps was now dead, and it wasn't too hard believing that whatever was in those bags had been responsible for the deaths of him and his brother. But, from everything I knew about them, the Phippses were just run-of-the-mill street punks who dreamt of the big league but would never get there as prison or unrealistic dreams would get in the way of this aspiration.

It all kept coming back to the bags. Yet they'd hardly been mentioned in the transcripts of his arrest interview, and it also mentioned that Phipps had said he'd seen the bags in plain sight. But Simeon had just told me Phipps had said the bags were hidden under the front passenger seat. He'd also alluded to the fact the car had been stolen because the brothers were paid to do so. Mullins had told me the woman whom the car was registered to had initially been upset at the loss of the car but had become almost unconcerned about the missing bags. It all added up to something not adding up.

Mickey was back in his bar. I was back in the office and had brought up Louis Phipps' record from the PNC. I reread the details of what passed for his criminal career. It was still as underwhelming as before. Nowhere was there any evidence he was a criminal mastermind in training and I didn't doubt that, had he lived longer, he would have ended up in jail for a long stretch or would end up dead, but not from the gun of a top-notch assassin.

I was going to have to talk to Ms Debbie Frost to get her view of events. Before doing so I went into the PNC to see what, if anything, was known about her.

Deborah Anne Frost was 33 and had an address in Chelsea. She had a flat in Mulberry Walk, which was quite close to the King's Road. She was a graduate in Politics and History from New College, Oxford, where she'd gone after attending public school, and she was currently employed as a senior research analyst for the Conservative Party, where she'd been since leaving Oxford, apart from a short spell in a Merchant Bank in the City.

I sat forward when I saw that. That meant she would be

close to the epicentre of power as the research department was based in Millbank, a goal kick's distance from the Houses of Parliament. Her duties included preparing briefing packages for Government ministers on issues they were contemplating legislating upon. This was a very sensitive position and would have involved her being vetted by the security service when the Tories won the 2010 election to ascertain whether she could be trusted with top secret material, though there were no details of the vetting in her Special Branch file. I was interested in politics myself and could imagine a job like this being intellectually stimulating, particularly if you subscribed to the political philosophy behind what you were doing. But how many of them actually subscribed to any real political beliefs?

She had no criminal record and her credit rating was excellent. Her father was a small businessman and Tory councillor back home in Witney, Oxfordshire, and her mother ran a small shop selling knitwear and fabrics in the town centre. She had a younger brother who'd been in the army and had served in Afghanistan but he'd left when his time was up and he was currently back in the UK working for his father.

Debbie was engaged to someone named Darren Ritchie, whom she'd met at Oxford, and who was listed as being a merchant banker working for a prestigious American firm in Cheapside. He also had the same address as Debbie, so even I could deduce they were living together. He too had no record or any major debts beyond having a mortgage. They were almost the perfect modern Tory couple. Yet her name had come up in connection with a car theft and a petty criminal who was supposed to be involved in blackmail. And he was dead. Time to talk to Ms Debbie Frost.

I phoned her office and was told she was in a meeting. I left my number and asked her to call when she was able to. She returned my call twenty minutes later. I explained who I was and asked if she'd be available for a routine conversation concerning the loss and recovery of her car. She said she would be happy to but didn't want to do it at work so could we meet elsewhere. I suggested a coffee shop at the top end of Victoria Street and we agreed to meet there at 3pm.

She was there when I arrived. I recognised her from the picture on her file. She was a stunningly attractive woman. She had dark hair, and lots of it, cascading past her shoulders, as well as eyes a man could drown in. She was wearing a dark coloured business suit and a pale blue blouse, with a white silk scarf hanging loosely from her shoulders. There was a copy of *Cosmopolitan* on the table in front of her. Everything about her oozed style and class and she projected herself with all the confidence gained from an expensive education, plus mixing with the elite of the political classes.

The waitress was just bringing her a latte so I ordered a tea and sat opposite her. I introduced myself as the Special Branch officer who'd called earlier and repeated why I wanted to talk to her.

"You reported a car being stolen, didn't you?" I began.

"Yes, I did." Her voice was calm and assured.

"You reported it as being stolen from a car park by Waterloo station."

"That's right. I parked it there as I was at a meeting nearby. When I returned I saw the car had been taken and I phoned 999."

"You initially said you were concerned about the loss of the bags in the car, but I was told that changed. Why was that?"

"I was concerned about losing my handbag because I thought it had my purse and credit cards and all that, but it didn't. They were in my other bag, so all I lost was some junk really." She sounded relieved.

"What about the other bag? I believe there was also an

official looking briefcase taken as well. What was lost there?"

"Oh, nothing really, just some old papers, memos, notes made from talks with various people in the office, a few ideas for what we need to talk about at forthcoming meetings, that kind of thing. There was nothing of any value and most of it was probably going to be shredded anyway, so once I was told it was all junk I was less bothered about the loss. If whoever stole the car was hoping they'd get something from what was in the bag, they'd be very disappointed as it was of no value."

"Who told you it was all junk?"

"I reported it missing to the office but was told not to worry as there was nothing of any value in the case, just mainly stuff nobody cares about too much."

"No official files or photos, anything of that kind?" I ventured.

"Photographs? No, nothing like that. Why do you ask?"

"I'm just trying to ascertain what's missing. The bags have never been recovered and we need to keep a record of missing property in case it materialises later."

"Fair enough." She sipped her latte. From the look on her face she liked the taste.

"Would whoever took the briefcase have been able to open it easily?"

"Highly unlikely. The lock was especially made for that type of bag to give extra protection against theft. It's a make very popular with businessmen who carry sensitive documents with them when they travel. To force it open would cause real damage to the whole case and significantly detract from any resale value it might have. They'd need the key to open it and I had it on me."

I'd heard earlier that Phipps had been able to open the briefcase and what he'd seen had formed the basis of his assertion that the contents were going to make him rich. Why would Debbie Frost maintain she had the key with her?

"So, who did the bags actually belong to?"

"Me," she relied instantly. "They're my bags."

"Your bags," I repeated. "I was under the impression the briefcase belonged to someone else, possibly your boss?"

"No, no. They're both mine, or were till someone swiped them both with my car. But at least I got my car back. That's far more important."

"You know someone was charged with stealing your car, don't you?"

"Yes." She smiled, though I got the impression it was a forced smile. "A couple of wastes of space who I think were identified from their fingerprints."

"That's true, they were. Funny thing is, despite the loss to the victim, car crime doesn't usually require someone being fingerprinted, or a DCI ordering it to be done."

"Well, whatever, the culprits were identified and punished. That's all I care about."

She took another sip of her latte. I began to get a sense I was about as welcome as dandruff. She'd gone from answering questions politely to almost surly.

"Do you remember getting a call from someone called Louis Phipps?"

"Who?"

"Louis Phipps. He's one of the two men who took your car. I'm told he phoned and offered you the chance to buy back what he'd taken from you."

"No, I don't think so. No one contacted me about it. The only contact I received was from the police when they told me my car had been found in Herne Hill. Who told you about my being contacted?" She seemed concerned.

"Oh, perhaps I misheard. I thought I heard you'd been contacted by someone about the theft."

"No," she said firmly. "Nobody contacted me about the car except the police."

This also contradicted what Simeon had said earlier today. Interesting.

"Also, I heard the bags were lying on the passenger seat in

the front of the car. Bit careless, isn't it, considering who you work for and what you do?"

"The bags were not visible. They were under the front passenger seat. Anyone looking in the car window would not have been able to see them at all," she stated with certainty.

"You're quite sure about that?"

"Definitely. I placed them under the seat myself."

This was also at odds with all I'd heard earlier. Curious.

"So you've no idea why it was your car that was stolen?"

"It's brand new, a Prius. For a criminal it would mean the chance to unload it for a profit. That's why. I was just unlucky. My car was in the right place but at the wrong time because those two crooks were there and took it. But, aside from a broken side window, they didn't cause any damage to it. I was worried they would."

She seemed certain in her answers. What she was saying, however, was at odds with what I'd been told earlier by people who knew Louis Phipps. I was feeling somewhat bemused.

"Did you ever get the sense your car was targeted? I mean, there were quite a lot of cars in that car park, including some quite high powered top of the range models, but the two guys went straight for yours, which wasn't even on the ground floor."

"Targeted? What are you getting at? You mean the person who stole my car deliberately singled it out?"

"That's just what I mean."

"No, I didn't. I was just unlucky. Those scumbags saw my car and took it. That's what I think."

"Okay." I nodded my agreement. "Anything else you want to add to what you've already said?"

"No, I don't think so. Is that it? I really should be going back now."

I agreed I'd nothing else to ask her and I thanked her for her time and cooperation. I stood up as she rose and left the café. I then realised she'd left me with the bill.

*

Walking back to the Yard I replayed the conversations I'd had that day and they all led me to the conclusion that this case was not as straightforward as it had initially seemed. Debbie Frost was adamant she'd lost nothing of value in what to her was simply an unfortunate random car theft, yet Louis Phipps was convinced he'd come across something that would make him rich. He'd also told Simeon he'd stolen the car at the behest of someone who wanted the car but who ended up just taking whatever it was from a bag.

Whatever, the fact was that Louis and Paulie had been shot dead two nights back and I knew two things: that Phil Gant had pulled the trigger, though proving it would be a challenge, and that somehow it was all connected to whatever was in those two bags.

What had Louis and Paulie Phipps got themselves into?

I was pondering everything I'd heard today. The only certainty was that Louis and Paulie Phipps were dead. I knew; I saw it happen. I'd initially expressed disbelief they could have done anything that would involve someone unknown hiring a triple-A assassin. But, talking to Gant and learning he had indeed been hired to kill the Phipps brothers, and his being in proximity when they died, had removed some of my early scepticism. I'd since learned from two of his friends that Louis Phipps believed he was going to get rich from what he'd found in a car it would appear he'd been paid to steal for someone. I'd been told he'd contacted the owner of the car he'd stolen but Debbie Frost had denied any contact at all. Why would she do that? Or had Simeon been lying to me? He had nothing to gain by lying. He was a friend of Phipps, or at least someone he had drugs in common with.

I needed to know more about Debbie Frost, and I knew the very person to ask.

I met him in a pub near to where *New Focus* had its offices.

Richard Clements had been just about to leave work when I phoned him around four thirty and he agreed to my request to meet in an hour for a quick chat and a beer. I was still technically on holiday so I permitted myself a pint of London Pride whilst he stuck to lager.

I sat opposite him. His hair had been cut though it was still quite long and his beard was now almost designer stubble. Was the George Michael look coming back? I hoped not. It amused me knowing he was now the son-in-law of my boss Smitherman and, given the polarity of their politics, I could imagine the conversations around the dinner table. It amazed me even more that a friendship of sorts had evolved between us over the past six months. At one time, as students, I'd wanted to stick his head down a toilet, preferably an unflushed one, but now I was sharing a beer with him. Times change.

When I'd phoned earlier I asked if he knew someone named Debbie Frost and he said he did. Or rather knew who she was as they'd met at various political gatherings he'd covered for his magazine. He'd said he could get more information on her in a little while and he said he had. I began by asking what he knew about her.

"She's a looker, I know that much." He grinned lecherously. "What's she done to get herself on Special Branch radar?"

"Her car was stolen a while back and there's some issue concerning the contents of the bags she lost. But, before any of that, what can you tell me about her?"

"What, Miss hoity-toity Sloane Ranger wannabe? She's a couple of decades too late. She'd been around when Lady Di was still alive, I've no doubt she'd have been one of her little coterie of fawning acolytes."

"What else?"

"I've met her a few times, usually when I've been at a press conference. She's sometimes involved with putting them on. I was at the last Tory Party conference and she was helping out at a fringe meeting about Civil Liberties, if memory serves. I attended that meeting. Usual blue rinse Tories there, arguing about what Civil Liberties we should have in the UK. In other words, just the liberty to get rich by any means possible." He laughed at his own witticism. "She followed me into the café afterwards and asked what a magazine like the *New Focus* might be doing at the conference. We had a bit of a chat but not much else. It was all very friendly."

"What does she actually do? I know she works for Conservative Party research."

"Yeah, she does. She's something to do with preparing policy briefs for ministers in the areas of Defence and Civil Liberties. She's at that kind of level. Very pushy, very ambitious; sees herself as the next iron lady leader of the Party. Every time a Tory safe seat comes up her name goes forward but she's yet to be selected for one. I hate what she stands for but, when you look at some of the idiots on their front bench, she'd certainly be an improvement on what's already there."

"Is she Cabinet material?"

"God yeah. I can imagine her as Home Secretary. That would make her the titular Head of MI5. That'd be interesting, all those spooks answering to her." He smiled at the thought.

"What about her background, you know anything about that?"

"Usual high flying Tory pedigree. Went to some flash public school, seamlessly onto Oxford, then a cushy job in the Tory Party. Parents had money. She's probably never had to work for anything in her life. Meritocracy still lives in the Tory Party." Sarcasm abounded in his tone. "There's no doubt she'll get a safe seat, sooner rather than later I suspect. People like her use their position as a stepping stone to a seat in the House. The only thing likely to get in the way is her views."

"Meaning what, exactly?"

"She holds very right-wing views, even for the Tories, on just about everything, especially race and Europe. No more immigration to the UK, especially non-white immigrants, let's get out of the European Union, Britain for the British, that kind of Little Englander mentality. You should hear them at their Party conference. She hasn't caught up with the fact the world has moved on quite considerably in the past few decades. I suspect, had she been old enough, she'd have been in Portsmouth in 1982 waving goodbye to the task force on its way to that useless lump of rock in the South Atlantic."

I thought I'd got some sense of what her political slant was from the way she'd referred to the Phipps brothers and the tone of voice describing them.

"What's your interest in her, Rob? She been stealing the silver in the Commons?"

"Her name came up in a case recently. The person who stole her car a few months ago wound up dead in suspicious circumstances the other night and I'm looking into the case, given who she is and what she does."

"Is there a connection between the two things?" He looked puzzled.

I debated how much to tell him. I decided to go with my gut instinct. My instinct had been wrong before but I thought I could trust it this time.

"This is strictly between us and completely off the record. We clear?"

He nodded his assent.

"Did you see yesterday's *Standard*? Two guys shot dead in Bayswater Monday night?"

He nodded. "Yeah, nasty business."

"They're the ones who stole her car. I think I know who killed them but I'd rather not say just yet. What I do know is that the two guys, brothers, were a pair of losers, in and out of trouble their whole lives. They steal a car a couple of months back, though, and soon after they get shot dead. The car just happens to belong to Ms Debbie Frost. According to one of the two guys, there was something in the car that was going to make him rich, yet the car owner says there was nothing in the car and, soon after, both guys are shot dead."

"Christ!" Clements exclaimed. "You saying she had them killed 'cause they ripped off her car?"

"No, nothing like that. She's not a suspect. She just happened to be the owner of the car they stole. I'm just trying to ascertain what was in the bags that were stolen because I think whatever was there was a factor in their killings, but Ms Frost was not very helpful in that regard."

"So, who did kill those two?"

"I was there but didn't see who did it."

"You were there? You saw it go down?"

"Yeah, I did. I saw someone earlier who's a known killer. A little while later the Phippses are shot dead. I'm almost certain it was him but I didn't see him do it and I can't prove it. MI5 spoke to him and he was cleared so it's a dead end for the moment."

"MI5 don't normally get involved in routine killings like this, do they?" Clements was lapsing into investigative journalist mode. He could sense something in what he was being told.

"That's right, they don't. Which is why it's strange that the person concerned should be seen by the security service."

"Is this why you were asking about mercenary soldiers yesterday?" His eyebrows went up, sensing something in the air. I sipped my beer and didn't reply. He continued, "What kind of killing was it, some kind of contract hit? If these guys on the front of yesterday's paper are the losers you say they are, who'd want to bump them off like that? Sounds like a cold-blooded killing to me."

"It was. Straightforward murder as far as I'm concerned. CID is investigating but it's unlikely they'll get to the bottom of it. As I said, I'm sure I know who killed them but I don't think that person will ever be brought to justice. I'm looking into what it was that might have got them shot in the first place."

"Don't suppose you wanna spill your suspicions to a poor humble hack?" He looked hopefully at me, like a dog expecting to be given a treat.

"For the moment, no. That stays with me."

He sat back and sipped some more beer.

"You could help me out, though," I said.

"Oh yeah, how?"

"Find out all you can about Debbie Frost. You know, who her friends are, her habits, where she goes, how she spends her evenings, where she does her shopping, what she eats for breakfast. Anything like that would be a big help. I can't do it as this isn't a Special Branch matter yet, and I'm supposed to be on holiday, but anything you can dig up, I'd be grateful."

"I can do that. I know one or two people I can grill about the lovely Ms Frost. I can probably have something for you by this time tomorrow, maybe even sooner."

"Thanks for that." I gave him my mobile number.

Back in the office I poured a coffee from a pot that had probably been made before I left to go on holiday. It was still warm and tasted like sour chicory.

I made notes about what I knew. It didn't take long. The only certain fact was that two men were dead. I suspected I knew their killer but had no proof. I'd learned from talking to people who knew him that Louis Phipps was expecting to make money from the proceeds of his crime but the car owner had said she'd lost nothing of value. The bags in her car had never been recovered either. Rhodes had said Gant was after the Phippses for blackmail but I suspected they thought blackmail meant letters delivered to coloured people. Gant was a top-notch hitman and I wondered what the real reason for his involvement was.

There seemed to be lots of pieces of information

floating about but I couldn't seem to connect any of them together. Something didn't make sense here and I didn't know what.

It then dawned on me that, when I'd arrived at Mickey's bar, Gant had seen me enter and contacted someone with a description of the person entering, and it had come back as me. Who might Gant know who also knew who I was? The only person who came to mind was Gavin Dennison, who would almost certainly know of someone like Gant because of his work at *Prevental*. Could it have been him Gant called?

I dialled *Prevental* and asked for Gavin Dennison. I gave the name Phil Gant. After a few seconds I heard Dennison's voice.

"Phil, How you doing, mate? What do you need?" I rang off. He'd not be able to trace the call.

So it was him.

I was curious about what was in the two bags. I suspected it was whatever the bags contained that had got the Phipps brothers killed but, without Gant or the bags, I couldn't say for certain. There was also the fact that a DCI and MI5 had been involved after the Phippses' arrests.

It all added up to one thing. I was confused.

Smitherman was still at his desk despite it being early evening. He was just back from a meeting with several senior officials at the Home Office. As Head of Special Branch the demands on his time were considerable, which was one reason why his job was unappealing to me and I wouldn't take it if begged on bended knee by the Queen and offered a fortune in gold bullion.

I knocked and entered his office. He looked up from his laptop.

"I see enough of you when you're supposed to be here," he said almost resignedly.

"I've been looking into the Phipps case the other night. Something doesn't add up."

"What might that be?" He stopped what he was doing and gestured for me to sit. I did.

I told him what I'd been doing over the past two days, where I'd been and whom I'd spoken to, though for the moment I left out his son-in-law. Smitherman was still under the impression we were not friends, which I was happy to go along with. He listened intently whilst I spoke, looking directly at me. He nodded and took a sip of water when I finished.

"You do know this isn't our case, don't you? CID's handling it. There's nothing so far to suggest this is anything other than an ordinary murder investigation."

"Yeah. I spoke to DI Harrow outside the bar. I told him who the shooter was but so far as I know, he's still walking about free as a bird. I think the two guys were killed because of what they found in the bags they took from the car they stole."

"Do you have any idea what that might be?"

"Nope, but it was supposed to be really valuable, according to people I spoke to earlier today."

"You say you also spoke to Debbie Frost."

"Yeah, this afternoon."

"You do know who she is and what she does, don't you?"

"I should do. I spoke to her about it." I grinned. He didn't.

"This is serious, Rob. As I said yesterday, Gant is untouchable unless we get solid evidence that puts him at the scene. Yes, I know you saw him about ten minutes before the shootings, but you didn't actually see him shoot, did you? We both know what any half competent brief would make of that one in court." He shook his head. "I know about Gant. He's been on the watch list of the security services for a while but, so far as is known, he's never operated in this country. He has no form in the UK so, without proof, or at least a better than reasonable suspicion of any involvement or complicity in these deaths, we can't move against him."

"What doesn't make any sense to me is why someone like

Gant went after the Phippses. I know of some of the kills he's done and there's usually some issue of principle or state security involved. Hard to imagine either of those covering killing Louis and Paulie Phipps. I still think it comes down to what was in the bags. It's whatever was there that got those two killed and I think CID are gonna be chasing their own tail on this. I don't suppose they've found anything yet?"

"Nothing I've heard of. There were no witnesses other than you and your friend and you've both been cleared of any involvement. They've been investigating but haven't come up with anything substantial in the way of leads."

"They won't either. We both know who did this."

"You could be right, but I don't approve of my officers breaking down doors to look for whatever it was you were after, especially when they're not even following up a Branch case, and even more so when they're with someone who's not even a police officer any longer. Did you even find anything to justify what you did?"

"Found a God-awful mess, that's about it."

"But nothing substantial."

I shook my head. "No. If Phipps has hidden whatever he found in that case, it's not in the flat."

Smitherman sat at his desk and looked at me. I knew he was pondering whether to praise my diligence and dedication to duty during what, last Friday evening, had begun as a week's holiday, or threaten me with a written warning for not following standard police procedure. I was hoping he would come down on the side of the former. He exhaled. I was in luck.

"I'm going to give you some leeway on this. We've not had any complaints about heavy-handed police conduct so I've only your word it occurred. I'm assigning this aspect of the case to you, looking into the blackmail angle, so you're not likely to tread on CID's toes, especially as they're looking for a likely suspect for the killing. You were even at the scene of the crime and, since then, you've uncovered a few things, so I'd like you to follow them up. If there's any evidence of anyone in Government being blackmailed, it's important I'm told as I'll have to bring MI5 into the picture. You understand?"

I said that I did.

"So, what's the first step?"

"I'm going to focus on finding out exactly what Phipps was supposed to have found that he was going to use for leverage against whoever. That'll mean going into Phipps' life in detail, finding out who he's been hanging out with and where, and seeing what they know about this. It's likely he dumped the bags somewhere but if he kept whatever was in them, then it has to be stored somewhere. That's what I'll have to try and find first."

"Good luck with that."

"As we're now looking into this case, could you have a word with your pal, Warren. Ask him why MI5 interviewed Phipps about a car theft?"

"Given the car's owner, and the position she holds, it's not a big surprise they'd want to know what's happening, but I'll see what he knows."

Back on the PNC looking at the life and times of Louis Phipps yet again. I only knew him for a few hours and I'd developed a healthy contempt for him. For someone who was essentially a nonentity whilst alive, he was taking up a lot of my time now he was dead.

I was interested in the timeline relating to the events leading up to his untimely demise. He'd stolen Debbie Frost's car on January 18th and been arrested three days later. It seemed odd that his interview had been partly conducted by MI5. That wasn't the norm for what looked like routine car theft. He was charged and bailed to appear in court on March 26th where he'd received a suspended sentence. That was six weeks back. In that time whatever he'd taken from the car had not been recovered and it was my belief that the failure to recover this item had led someone to hire Gant. What had he been up to in the meantime?

The only address listed was the one Mickey and I had searched earlier and we'd not found anything out of place, in the sense of not belonging there. Maybe we'd not looked closely enough.

I scanned all the entries for him. I was familiar with his unimpressive list of criminal misadventures. I wanted to know more about anyone he was known to be close to, anyone who could give me an idea of what the Phipps brothers had been doing lately. I don't know why I was surprised but the file listed their mother as still being alive and living in Kentish Town. I wondered if she'd been notified about the death of her sons. Only their mother could possibly love the likes of the Phipps brothers.

I noted a few names and addresses and decided to make a start on them that evening.

The Phippses lived in Brixton and one friend listed had an address nearby so that was the place to start. I was looking for someone named Cyril Nwojo, aged 22, who was listed as having been arrested on drugs charges alongside Louis Phipps. I drove back to Brixton and parked in Loughborough Road, near to where I was looking for. The house was one in a line of terraced houses and, from the outside, every bit as seedy as where Phipps lived, down at heel and with a downwind air of squalor and urban decay. Gentrification had evidently not extended to this road. Parked in front of the house was a car with a number of its tyres slashed and the windscreen cracked sufficiently to prevent anyone driving it.

I rang the bell. The door was answered almost immediately by a surly looking, dishevelled black man with unfocused eyes and wearing a faded Bob Marley T-shirt and a pair of discoloured jeans. He looked about as pleased to see me as he would seeing a hooded member of the Klan at the door.

"Yeah, what you want?" He spoke almost perfect estuary English.

"Police. Looking for Cyril Nwojo," I said showing him my ID.

"You Drugs Squad?"

"Special Branch. That's a step upwards in class from what you're used to dealing with."

The man stared at me for the regulation few seconds so I could take in that, so far as he was concerned, a visit from Special Branch wasn't any big deal.

He then stepped aside. I entered.

"Go straight on ahead." He nodded towards the end of the passageway. I did.

We went into the kitchen. He turned the music off. There was a pleasant smell of whatever had been cooked recently permeating the air. The dog lying on a basket in the corner simply turned over when I entered. Some watchdog.

"So, what do you want with me? I ain't done anything." He sounded nervous.

"You're a friend of Louis Phipps," I began.

"Yeah, I am. What's he been up to now?"

"That's what I'm hoping you can tell me. Louis's in a spot of bother concerning a car he stole. It seems he also stole something from that car that's very important and could land him in more trouble than he's currently in. It's very important we find what he's taken. I can't talk to Phipps himself just yet so, as you're his friend, perhaps you can enlighten me. When did you last see him?"

He pursed his lips as though internally struggling with whether to answer my question. His better half won out.

"Sometime last week. He was staying nearby and dropped in."

"How did he seem to you?"

"Nervous and agitated, he was worried about something."

"Did he tell you what about?"

Nwojo looked pensive and distracted. His eyes flickered back and forth, as though he was thinking hard. It didn't appear as though this was something he did on a regular basis.

"Look, man," he finally said, "I don't wanna get involved in this. Louis said it was heavy, something about his being blackmailed into doing something for some police guy and it not working out."

"Whoa, back up," I blurted out. I was surprised at what he'd said. This was wholly unexpected. The blackmail I thought I was looking into was Louis Phipps on someone else. But this man had just said that it was the other way around. What was going on here?

Cyril Nwojo looked as though he wished he'd never spoken. He was tapping his fingers nervously on a packet of cigarettes. He opened the packet, took one out and lit it.

"I shouldn't have said that. Oh God, this is intense, man."

I sat down at the table and looked directly at him.

"Well, you said it and I want to know the rest. So, I want you to start at the beginning and tell me everything Louis Phipps told you when you last saw him. This is important, more so than you could possibly realise."

Cyril Nwojo looked up after a few moments' thought.

"You've gotta keep my name outa this. He told me all this in confidence, y'know? If he knows I talked to the police about it ..." His voice tailed off.

"I promise I won't say a word to Louis about this. Not one word."

This would be a very easy promise to keep as I didn't know any mediums. Just as well as I didn't believe in them anyway.

"Alright." Cyril stubbed out his cigarette. "He came here one night last week, Wednesday I think, and was, y'know, quite agitated. I asked him what's the matter, and he said that, a while back, he didn't say when exactly, he got pulled over by police for something. But instead of taking him to the station, he got took someplace private, he didn't say where. This police officer says he knows all about what Louis and his brother Paulie have been doing and was gonna drop them right up to their necks in it."

Simeon had said Phipps had been asked to steal the car, but Cyril Nwojo was now saying this was as a result of Phipps being coerced into doing so.

"What had they been doing?" I interrupted him.

"Oh, the usual; stealing anything not nailed down, moving stolen goods, bit of dope dealing, getting into fights, stuff like that. Louis's always got something on the go." He almost smiled.

"He buys his drugs from Simeon, doesn't he?"

"You know about Simeon?" His eyes opened slightly wider.

"Everyone does," I lied, "so, if that's where you buy from, go someplace else as he's under constant police observation. Anyway, go on."

"Alright, as I says, this police guy, apparently he tells Louis he's in a position to do him a favour."

"Like what?"

"He said that, if Louis could do a job for him, he'll ignore what he's been up to and forget all about it if it works out."

"What if he'd refused?"

Cyril stared at me as though I were an idiot. "What do you think? The guy tells him he'll throw the fucking book at him if he doesn't cooperate."

"I see. So what was this job?"

"He wanted Louis to steal a car for him."

I had the uncomfortable feeling I knew where this was going.

"What car?" I asked neutrally.

"Never said. He just said about stealing it."

"Steal it from where?"

"Car park by Waterloo. He was to steal it and take it someplace. He never said where."

"Did he have to steal any particular car or the first one he came to?"

"He was told which one he was to lift."

"Why steal this car? What was so special about it?"

"This bloke wanted something that was in the car. That's why that particular car."

This meant Debbie Frost hadn't been completely honest when she said there was nothing of any value in her car. She'd either had, or was holding onto, something this person wanted very much. This was becoming intriguing. Another talk with Ms Frost was now on the horizon.

"What happened afterwards?"

"Bloke comes over to look at what Louis stole. Seems he liked what he found in the car. He takes something and tells Louis to go dump the car somewhere. Louis does and, a few days later, he and Paulie are arrested. But, the thing is, he said he'd been told that, even if he gets nicked, he won't go down for it. Bloke was sure about that. Louis gets slipped some money for his troubles."

"Think carefully about this. Did Louis ever tell you what it was this police officer wanted?"

"Yeah. Something about a briefcase. Guy looks in it, takes something out and puts it back in the car and tells Louis to go dump the car."

Nwojo had the haunted expression of someone who'd just been told his ride to the gallows was outside waiting. It was a look of almost frozen terror, as though he didn't believe what he was actually being told or was telling me. But there was no stopping now.

"And that's what Louis did?" I ventured, knowing this wasn't what had gone down.

"Ah, not quite. Louis dumps the car alright but he keeps the bags that were there 'cause he thought he could make some bread from what was in them."

"Did he say what this was?"

"No, not to me, man."

"What did he do with these cases?"

"Dunno. He never said."

I'd been a police officer long enough to recognise a lie when it appeared. Everything about Cyril Nwojo suggested an economy with the truth. For the moment I left it alone.

"What happened after that?"

"Didn't say much. Something about phoning someone from a number he took from the handbag and that person threatening him, but not much else."

"Did he say who this person was? Did he mention any names?"

"Not to me, he didn't."

"Is there anything else you can tell me about this?"

"Yeah. He was also uptight because someone had threatened to kill him so he wasn't staying at his place, like, he crashed someplace else to get away."

"Did he say anything about being shot at?"

"Yeah," he perked up, as though this was the exciting bit. "Yeah, he says some dude appears from across the street and shoots at them, y'know, him and Paulie, but he didn't get them. Paulie was shitting himself, man." He laughed at the thought of what he'd said.

"Did he say if he thought the shooting was connected to the car theft?"

"No, I don't think he connected the two things up. I think he just thought he'd pissed someone else off. Ain't the first time someone's tried to top him."

"And you've not seen or heard from Louis Phipps since last Wednesday."

"Nope, not a thing."

"Where would he stay if he didn't stay at his own place?"

"I don't know." He shook his head. "He didn't stay here. That's all I know. He just left and I ain't seen him since. I think he still owes Simeon money and it don't do to owe Sim."

I sat back in the chair and thought for a moment. Was Cyril being honest with me or was he covering up for his friend?

"Think very carefully, Cyril; are you sure Louis Phipps didn't say what he did with the two bags from the car?" I asked slowly and forcefully.

"Yeah, really, he didn't tell me anything about that."

Short of pinning him to the wall and slapping him around a little, I didn't think I'd get any more out of Cyril Nwojo at this time. For the moment I was done.

"Is there anyone else Phipps might have talked to about this? Any other friends he'd let in on the secret?"

Cyril rattled off a few names and I wrote them down. Thanking him for his time I got up to leave and, whilst doing so, told him in no uncertain terms that, should he whisper anything about our little talk to another person, I'd make his life more miserable than it already was.

It was now 9.40. Back in the car I considered what Cyril Nwojo had told me. It was looking as though Louis Phipps had been telling the truth about what he'd found in the car. But what was intriguing me was learning that, according to Nwojo, Louis Phipps had been pressured into doing what he'd done by a police officer who wanted whatever was in the two bags. This had sinister undertones indeed and I wasn't liking where this was heading. For the moment I decided to forget about the other names on the list and go ruin Debbie Frost's evening for her.

I drove across Vauxhall Bridge, turned left and followed a bus along Grosvenor Road which fed into the Embankment. Turning into Oakley Street, I stopped just before the King's Road and parked in an empty space. I crossed the road and walked up to the junction of Mulberry Walk. Her flat was on the second floor of number 9, which was the penultimate house in what was a short road. There were no lights on.

I dialled her landline number from my mobile but went straight to voicemail. I declined leaving a message. Did I want to risk waking her up?

Deciding not to bother, I'd just turned to walk back to my car when a taxi pulled up by the junction with The Vine and Mulberry Walk. I saw three people disembark. Two were males, one considerably bigger than the other. I shrewdly guessed that one of the two was the live-in boyfriend but I couldn't see faces clearly in the dark. The other person was Debbie Frost. Under the street lighting I could see her shock of black hair cascading around her shoulders. The smaller of the two men paid the taxi driver and it pulled away. They went up the stairs to the front door and entered.

The taxi was waiting by the main King's Road when I tapped on the window. I showed the driver my ID and he wound down the window.

"The people you've just dropped off back there, where'd you pick them up from?"

"Somewhere along Piccadilly, mate, don't remember where exactly. "

"Nearer which end, Marble Arch or the Circus?"

"Marble Arch end, probably just past Green Park Tube."

"Had they booked the ride in advance? "

"No, they were on the pavement waving for a taxi as I passed them."

"I don't suppose you heard what they were talking about."

"No, sorry, wasn't really listening to them."

"Okay, thanks." He wound up the window and turned left into the Kings Road.

I wasn't sure what use this information was but it was better to know than not know. She now had company and I suspected would be unreceptive to a nocturnal visit. I was still considering my options when I saw a man turning from Mulberry Walk into The Vine and walk towards the King's Road. He looked familiar but, across the road, in the dark, I couldn't make out who it was. He was looking straight ahead. At the corner he turned to look right and I saw who it was. Richard Rhodes. He was the bigger of the two men who'd just got out of the taxi with Debbie Frost.

But how would he know her? I didn't believe Debbie or her boyfriend were thinking of joining up to whatever armed conflict Rhodes would be engaging in once he'd finished making it safe for more Colombian cocaine to flood the streets of London, and it was a sure bet he wasn't taking soundings about seeking a safe Tory seat. Which left me wondering whether he was anything to do with what had happened to the Phipps brothers.

FOUR

Thursday

I WAS LOOKING AT the file on Richard Rhodes. He was 34 and an ex-soldier who I already knew had left the army before his contract was officially up. This was because he'd beaten a staff sergeant half to death in a brawl in barracks at Aldershot. To avoid a court martial he'd resigned his commission and walked away with a greatly reduced annuity. This was eight years back and, since then, he'd been a mercenary. It was listed that he'd seen service in several theatres of war where, officially, the UK had no ongoing military activity.

He was known to have seen service in Southern Africa, Chechnya, Lebanon and Afghanistan. His expertise included not just fighting battles against whoever he'd been hired to fight against, but also helping to train rookie soldiers, some not too many years on from suckling their mother's milk, to use firearms and in principles of military combat. He was suspected of having been involved directly in combat activity, including one particularly gruesome encounter in Lebanon where a building complex had been attacked and mostly destroyed. It later emerged that many women and children had been taking refuge, and had perished when the building was fired upon. This had led to international condemnation but Rhodes had denied being directly involved in that attack though he didn't deny being in the country assisting rebel forces.

He had one conviction. Just after leaving the army, he'd taken on a gang of skinheads outside a pub one evening and, despite being outnumbered eight to one, he'd put two in hospital with broken bones and multiple facial contusions, plus knocking one out stone cold, before the others ran away. Taking on eight yobs and winning. I shouldn't have been impressed but couldn't help it. He'd been fined only a token amount as the magistrates accepted his claim that he was the victim of an unprovoked assault.

And now he was working as a bodyguard to a Colombian bigwig, walking behind to make sure the man was able to ply his ignoble profession with minimum outside interference from anyone who had no business involving themselves with his.

I cross-referenced his name against Phil Gant and discovered that, as well as what was known about Lebanon, they'd also been in other areas of conflict simultaneously. Both had been in Afghanistan at the same time. Were they working together?

I checked his family line. He came from East London. His birth details revealed no mention of a father but his mother was alive and still living in the same area.

But I could find no link to Debbie Frost. I'd hoped his family line would somehow interlink with hers but it didn't. Which left me wondering what circles she moved in that would bring her into contact with the likes of a mercenary killer like Richard Rhodes. Time to visit Ms Frost again.

I was told by Debbie Frost's PA she was in a meeting with MPs and wouldn't be available until around late morning. I said I'd call back and rang off without leaving a name. In the interim I still had some addresses of people who were listed as being friends of Louis Phipps. This involved another visit to the Brixton area. I parked on the main road and spent a fruitless hour either knocking on doors where nobody answered, or talking to people who claimed they barely knew Louis Phipps. From one person I discovered that Louis Phipps dealt in soft drugs and was unreliable as a person. This wasn't exactly news to me. He claimed to know nothing about Phipps' involvement in a recent car theft and said he'd not seen him for a couple of months. Frustrated, I went back to the office.

There was a message on my desk telling me to call someone named Rudolf. Who? Did I even know of any Rudolfs apart from Santa's red-nosed reindeer? Then it dawned on me; this was Phipps' supposed landlord.

I dialled the number given. The same vacuous female who'd been there, Twinky, answered and did not seem thrilled to hear my voice. I asked for Rudolf and she slouched off to get him. Rudolf came to the phone. I identified myself.

"Oh yeah, thanks for getting back. I just had a friend of Louis's round here, that dude Simeon. He wanted to know where Louis was 'cause Louis owes him money. He wasn't happy."

"Okay, but why tell me?"

"He told me to tell Louis that, unless he pays him real quick, he's not gonna get back what he left at Simeon's place for safekeeping."

He paused for a moment.

"Some dude came by and searched his room. I told you about him, didn't I? Real heavy guy."

"What was it Phipps left with Simeon?" I was definitely interested in this.

"Never said. Just said that, unless he gets his bread, Phipps ain't getting his package back."

I was beginning to think. Could Simeon be holding what it was I'd been looking for the past couple of days? Had Simeon been lying to me yesterday?

"What package is this?"

"I don't know, but it appears that Phipps took some dope to sell and, 'cause he was skint, he left something with Simeon as security. And now Sim's saying Louis ain't getting it back unless Phipps squares things with him."

"How much does Phipps owe?"

"Didn't say but it'd probably be around five grand. That's about the usual amount."

I thought about this. At King's, lecturers bought drinks for students but none peddled dope to them. I briefly wondered if the concept of in *loco parentis* applied to university students.

"Where's Simeon now?"

"I'm guessing at college. He said that's where he'd be if Phipps showed up with his money."

"Whereabouts does he work?"

"Greenwich University. Psychology Department. He teaches there."

"Don't let on you've talked to me. I'm going to have a word with Mr Simeon. I do believe he wasn't absolutely truthful with me when last we spoke."

The Psychology Department was at Avery Hill, in Eltham. I raced there with the use of a police siren to facilitate the journey. I parked and entered the main office. There were students standing around the counter but I walked to the front of the queue. I was told that Mr Simeon Adaka had his offices in the building opposite but that he was likely to be teaching or in a tutorial with a student. I said I would wait and walked over to his block, having no intention of waiting for the likes of him.

I found Simeon's office and entered. He was talking to a young black woman who had books and papers scattered across a nearby desk. He did not look pleased to see me again.

"Mr Adaka, good morning," I said jauntily, "we need to talk."

"Can't you see I'm busy?" He sounded irritable.

"No, I can't," I stated flatly. "Let me make it very simple for you. Either we talk now or I'm going to arrest you on suspicion of."

"Okay, okay, man." He looked at the surprised woman. "Can we finish up in a little while? This won't take too long."

She gathered her books and papers into a pile and left

them on the table. She left, scowling at me as she went out of the room, muttering under her breath.

He was dressed somewhat smarter than he'd been yesterday, with a smart but casual blue open-neck shirt and dark trousers. Compared to in his flat, at least he was dressed. He fixed me with what I assume he thought was an evil eye. My dog had looked at me more scarily when I'd not had a biscuit for her.

"Ladies' man, eh, Sim? Can I call you that?"

"What you want now? If you're still looking for Louis, I ain't seen him since you came to my place yesterday."

"Yes, I am, but that's not why I'm here. A little bird tells me you're holding something for him. Am I right?"

"Rudolf. You spoke to Rudolf. That's how you and your partner found me, wasn't it? He's got a big mouth." He shook his head.

"Can the threats, Simeon. I want to know what it is you're holding for Louis Phipps as security for whatever drug deal went down."

Simeon stared at me for a few moments. From his expression I wasn't sure if he'd even heard what I'd said to him.

"Do the Governors at this place know about your sideline as a dealer? Your Faculty Head maybe? I wonder if they'd like to know?"

"Not a dealer, man. I just use a little and sell a bit."

"You sell to students?"

He didn't answer.

"As I thought. You're a dealer. For the moment, however, I've more important things to consider, and you can help with that."

"Like what?"

"I'm told Phipps gave you something to hold on to. I want to know what it is."

"It's not that special, just a kind of padded A4 envelope with lots of papers and some photos."

"You said yesterday Phipps was claiming that he'd come

across something that would make him rich. Is this what he was talking about?"

"I don't know. They just looked like newspaper cuttings and pictures of guys in uniforms."

"Uniforms?"

"Yeah, guys in military uniforms."

"You opened his package?" I enquired.

"No. He showed me a couple of them to convince me he had something of value for me to hold against the dope he took."

"Did he say what was so special about these pictures?"

"Not to me. Just said something about them having lots of value to the owner, and that the person owning them wouldn't want them out in the open."

Was this the source of Phipps' supposed blackmail? Could the person in any of those pictures be someone prominent in political life? This also raised the intriguing idea that Louis Phipps could even recognise someone prominent in political life. I doubted his newspaper reading extended much beyond topless women on page three.

"Were these what he took from that car he stole?"

"I'd guess so. Most other stuff he steals, he either fences or is more open about what it is."

"You're quite sure this material is what Phipps claimed was going to make him rich? He wasn't just stringing you along?"

"No, man, he was hot on this one. I'd never seen him so worked up and excited as he was for this. Phipps is usually full of shit about how this or that scheme was gonna make him a pile of bread, but he was pumped about this. This is the big one, he kept saying. This is gonna do it for me. That's what he said."

Simeon looked as though he believed what he was saying.

"Okay. Listen very carefully," I said in a serious tone. I was hoping to scare Simeon. "It's my belief that whatever's in that package is being used to blackmail someone in

Government and now some very nasty people out there are looking for it. Why do you think Phipps is hiding?"

"Phipps never said that."

"He didn't know. He thought the pictures and whatever else is there were only worth something to whoever it was who wanted them. He didn't realise the full extent of what he had, and now he has, he's gone into hiding. It's essential to remember who it was he contacted about returning the stuff he took. Did he say who it was he got in touch with?"

"No. It could be with the rest of the stuff in the package."

"Where's this package now?"

Simeon looked me in the eye. If I'd hoped to scare him, from his facial expression, I'd succeeded.

"Blackmail's a particularly heinous offence, carries a lot of years in prison. You holding on to whatever it is ties you into the conspiracy. That means serious prison time as well as losing your cushy little number here dealing drugs, sorry, I mean teaching psychology, and with a prison record you'll never get another teaching job either. You ready for all that, Sim? Does Louis Phipps really mean that much to you that you'll put your life on hold for him? Would he do that for you? I somehow don't think he would." This did the trick.

"It's at my place. I've put it somewhere safe."

That was what I wanted to hear.

"Okay, get your coat. Guess where we're going?"

"Oh, come on, man, I'm doing a tutorial. I ain't got time for that just now."

There was a jacket hanging behind the door. I slid it off the coat hanger and tossed it at Simeon.

"Make time. You don't really have a choice. What do you think this is, a democracy?" I smiled.

With an injudicious usage of the siren we managed to get to Simeon's house in Brixton in not too many minutes. He looked sullen most of the journey and said nothing, simply looked out the window. Was he dreaming of his nest egg disappearing?

I parked just along from his house.

"Let's go get the package, shall we?" I gestured towards his house.

He made a noise that sounded something like "Hmmph" and got out the car. I followed. The house still reeked of marijuana. We went through a grubby looking kitchen and into the garden. There was a dilapidated shed at the bottom. He unlocked the shed door and went to a shelf filled with paint tins. Taking a large pot of emulsion down, he opened the tin. It was empty save for a brown padded A4 envelope carefully folded around the inside. He took it out, flattened it down and passed it to me.

"This is it. This is what Phipps gave me to hold."

"Is this all of it?"

"It's all he gave me."

"Did this come with a briefcase or other bag?"

"No. Only this."

I felt the package. It felt like there were some sheets of paper in there and a few A5 size photographs.

"I'll take your word for it, but if I find out you've held anything back, that's an obstruction charge right there. That's on top of what I said earlier plus whatever charges the Drugs Squad decide to bring, plus a word in the ear of your college principal," I said plainly.

I went into the kitchen. It looked and smelled unappetising. I was glad I wasn't hungry. I'd sooner eat off my kitchen floor as it was cleaner than here.

"Don't forget, you never saw me today. It's important you say nothing about this to anyone." I held up the envelope. "As I said, some unpleasant people are probably looking for this."

"Oh, don't mention it, Officer. Pleased to be of service." He was clearly unhappy. "What am I gonna tell Phipps when he turns up with my money and asks for his package?" He sounded worried. I resisted telling him, if Louis Phipps did turn up, it would only be to haunt him.

"You're a bright bloke, you'll think of something." I left him fuming.

I got into my car. I didn't open the package immediately, deciding to wait until I got back to my desk when I could look at it under appropriate conditions.

It was now eleven forty, according to my watch. Should I call to see if Ms Frost was back at her desk? I thought I'd wait and call her from the office. As I started the car my mobile sounded.

"Rob, Richard Clements. You wanted some stuff on Debbie Frost," he said enthusiastically.

"I did. You found anything?"

"Oh yeah, have I got news for you." He sounded excited, as though he was lining up a hot date.

"That's good. When can I get it?"

"Meet me for lunch and it's yours, mate." It unnerved me that he called me mate. "Fancy going to The Clarence again?"

I agreed I did and we arranged to meet in an hour or so.

That gave me time to return to New Scotland Yard and park the car. I then went to my desk and inserted the A4 envelope in my drawer.

The Clarence is at the Trafalgar Square end of Whitehall. It's a busy pub at lunchtimes, with lots of civil servant types and tourists favouring it. It was here I'd met Clements when, on a previous case, I told him about my frustrated efforts to nail whoever it was killing people, and I'd given him a lead to follow with other, more resourceful journalists, and they'd certainly stirred the pot.

To this day I still believe my boss, DCI Smitherman, thinks it was me who gave Clements the tip which set the investigative ball rolling. He'd never asked me outright, but there was something about the way he looked at me when he spoke of it that suggested he thought I knew something.

I arrived ten minutes before Clements. I bought him a beer and a coffee for myself and sat at a table in the corner. He arrived a few minutes later.

"That for me?" He nodded at the pint. I agreed it was. He drained half the glass in one go.

He was still impeccably unkempt, wearing a white T-shirt advertising a sci-fi film I was vaguely aware of under his leather jacket and a pair of dark blue jeans. His sartorial elegance was almost certainly a source of irritation to his impeccably attired father-in-law, DCI Smitherman.

"So, Ms Frost. What have you got?"

"A ton of stuff, man. I asked a couple of friends who work for national dailies what they knew about her. They asked people who knew people who knew her, usual kind of incestuous circles politicos move in," he began. "She's well thought of and highly regarded at work, very competent and all that. Said to have more attitude than a sunstruck Armadillo. Gets good reports and tipped for the top. She's well to the right of the Tory Party, you aware of that? At work she's one of that clique of economic libertarians who regard Thatcher as a dangerous Liberal. But even that couldn't get her into Bullingdon because of her gender. That really wound her up."

"Huh? That a college?"

"No, the Bullingdon Society, an exclusive club at Oxford for the sons of the rich, as is Oxford generally, whose members delight in their bad behaviour; smashing up restaurants after expensive dinner parties, that sort of thing, and in flaunting their wealth. Most of them go on to achieve political office, almost always in the Tory Party. The current political elite have at least three ex-Bullingdon Society in its ranks."

"What did she do at Oxford? Who did she associate with?"

"The usual Hooray Henry types people like her get drawn

to. But, most of those she mixed with weren't just out for a good time; they were deeply political, very right wing. She was in a group called *White Britain* at Oxford, a kind of modern version of bodies like the old *League of Empire Loyalists,* real Rule Britannia stuff. They advocated things like all non-whites repatriated back to their homeland. If the BNP had a collective brain, it would be like this lot."

If she'd been vetted for her current post, this must be on record. I made a note to look it up when I got back to the office. Would this have been put down and excused as the inevitable excesses of gilded youth or noted as something more sinister?

"There were some real nasty types in her little crowd, a few of them Nazi sympathisers. They weren't Final Solution types but they definitely supported the social agenda of the Fascist Right; you know, no inter-marriage between black and white, banning all homosexuality, the weak and feckless not being allowed to reproduce, stuff like that. The far right's full of people who still believe those things. You should hear some of the fucking lunatics who go to the fringe meetings at their annual conferences. There's no evidence she ever held those kinds of views but she certainly mixed with people who did, and probably still do."

"And you say Debbie's been unable to get a safe seat to fight because she's an extremist?"

"Something like that. She's been close to being selected on two occasions but never made it to the final shortlist. Since leaving, sorry, *coming down* from Oxford," he scoffed, "she's worked in the City but is now working for the Tory Party. Something quite near the top of the totem pole, I'm told by someone who knows her."

"Yes, she is. Works in policy research, I believe. What about the boyfriend?"

"Darren. Some chinless yuppie City type, wouldn't know an honest day's work if it pissed on his shoes. He's in the Mergers and Acquisitions section of Karris and Millers, an

American investment group. They buy and sell companies all over the place. Makes a fucking fortune doing it."

"He's Oxford as well, isn't he?"

"Yeah, went there as a mature student straight from the army."

"The army? He's a soldier?" This surprised me.

"Used to be. Served a few years and then 'went up to Oxford'." He used his index fingers to make quotation marks. "He's been in corporate finance ever since."

"What did he do in the army?"

"That I don't know. He served in the South African army before he relocated to this country but I don't know what he did. I do know his family is quite well off and still believes in apartheid."

"He's South African? I thought apartheid was dead and buried now Mandela's president of the new Republic."

"Don't you believe it," he stated with certainty. "It still exists in some far-flung right-wing corners of the universe. You know how many Tories still mourn the loss of Empire? Did you know that, when India was granted independence in 1948, Enoch Powell refused to speak to Churchill for the next five years? Her guy, Darren, comes from a family that still has black servants and will only employ blacks as they believe they're socially and racially inferior to whites."

Could these be the circles where Richard Rhodes had come into contact with Debbie Frost? But, if so, how did this make Gant somehow part of this cosy little arrangement?

"Anything else about her?"

"Yeah, here's the real juicy bit." He drained his beer. "Did you know she had an affair with a leading Tory about a year or so back?"

"An affair?"

"Yup, with quite a high profile figure as well, my sources tell me. It all got quite nasty; threats and recriminations all over the place."

"Why?" I wasn't sure I wanted to know Court gossip but I listened anyway.

"Usual thing; he was much older than her, married, kids, promised to leave his wife and set up home with her. He reneges on the arrangement and she threatens to go public about her and him, go to the press and spill her guts, but it all got worked out and peace and harmony reigns in the Kingdom of Heaven again. There were even rumours the party leadership had to get involved to keep the peace between the warring tribes and that's how it got settled, and this stopped it getting into the press. But she was mightily pissed about it for a while."

"What about the boyfriend?"

"He moved out when it came to light but it's all lovey-dovey again now, or so it would seem."

"Who did she have the affair with?"

"That's just it. I don't know. My source either doesn't know or, if he does, isn't spilling the beans, so I can't tell you."

"Was it with someone at work?"

"All I know is that it was with a leading right-wing figure in the party. I don't know any names but I'd love to know. I'd run it in the *Focus*." He laughed. "Why should *Private Eye* get all the good scoops?"

"This have any impact at work? Any knock-on effects?"

"Don't know of any. She's still in the same department and, from what I hear, tipped for great things after the next election."

I mused over what I'd heard.

"Why do you need to know so much about this chick, anyway?" He grinned. "She sounds like an unpalatable right-wing bitch to me. I wouldn't touch her with a foot-long pole."

"She just seemed an unlikely person to be involved with what I'm looking into. Her file seemed pretty anodyne but, after speaking to her, I just got this sense something didn't fit, so I wanted to know more about her. Just as I said yesterday, this is off the record."

"Anything I've said of any use?"

"Don't know yet." I drained my lukewarm coffee, thanked him and left.

I was walking back to the office along Whitehall. At the traffic lights by Parliament Square I remembered Debbie Frost worked only a couple of hundred yards away along Millbank. I decided to pay her a visit.

At reception I identified myself and asked to speak with Debbie Frost. The woman behind the desk phoned her office and I was told to take the lift to the fourth floor. I did. I was met by Ms Frost's PA who took me to her office.

Debbie Frost didn't seem overly keen to see me from the look in her eyes. She kept typing for a few seconds and then stood.

"DS McGraw. To what do I owe this pleasure? Didn't I answer all your questions yesterday?" It sounded almost like a challenge.

She rose and walked to the window where a pair of small armchairs were neatly arranged opposite each other, with a glass top coffee table between them and copies of newspapers conspicuously displayed. She was elegantly dressed, wearing a pale green blouse with a necklace prominent over the neckline. She was also wearing a pair of tight dark trousers that suggested she had great legs. I tried not to stare too hard. She sat down and invited me to do so. I did.

"So, why do you need to see me again?"

On the way to her office I'd hummed and hawed as to how to approach this. In the end I went straight for it.

"I don't think you were completely honest with me when we spoke yesterday."

"Oh really," she sounded surprised. "I thought I was very specific with you."

"I thought that as well. But I've spoken to a couple of

people who've told me things that seem to contradict what you've said. So, I'd like to ask you once again. What exactly did you lose when your car was stolen?"

Her eyes narrowed and she looked out the window briefly. She had a look that suggested she'd sooner be having intense period pains than answering my questions.

"Look, I told you what it was. It was just a bag full of old papers that were due to be dumped. I lost nothing of any consequence and I'm surprised you can't accept that, I really am." She sounded almost exasperated, like a parent telling off a recalcitrant child for the umpteenth time.

"That's interesting because I have reason to doubt that, and I'll tell you why. Yesterday I spoke to two people who flatly contradict what you've said. They maintain that the person who took the bags from your car came across something that he was looking to cash in on, and it's my belief it's this that got the man concerned killed. I've had this from two separate sources, people who don't know each other and who have no reason to bullshit me, excuse my Latin. So, does that give you any indication why I'm sceptical about your story?"

"I'm sorry you feel that way, but my story remains the same." She was adamant. "All I lost was a bag full of old briefing documents and miscellaneous papers that were going to be shredded. If this person thought they were worth anything, he's sadly mistaken but good luck if he wants to try."

"Wanted to try, past tense now," I replied. "What exactly were these papers?"

"Just minutes from meetings, random notes, a few ideas for various things, some briefing notes for MPs who might be speaking in the House on a particular issue in response to what other parties might be saying. Basically, party documents we didn't want any longer. I can't reveal exact contents because the contents are a confidential party matter, I'm sure you understand."

"I'm not bothered about party matters. I'm interested in why someone would say what he found was valuable if you're certain it wasn't?"

"I can't answer that. I don't know." She looked out the window as she spoke.

"The person I'm talking about is someone who was, frankly, as stupid as they come. A petty crook destined for a life inside, yet this person maintains he made contact with you and you rebuffed him when he offered you your stuff back."

She shrugged her shoulders. "No one contacted me. What is it this person's supposed to have stolen from me that I'd want back so much?"

"That's what I'm trying to discover. The person concerned wasn't forthcoming about it and the people he told don't know either, which is why I'm asking you."

"I can only repeat what I said earlier. I didn't lose anything of any consequence."

"You said yesterday your office was unconcerned about the loss of the bags."

"That's right, they were. They assured me there was nothing valuable there so I wasn't to worry unduly about the theft."

"I see." I nodded. "And, to confirm what you also told me, nobody contacted you offering the chance to get back what was taken for a price."

"That's the situation."

She sounded plausible and I almost believed her. But there was something I couldn't put my finger on that was bothering me. It was time to raise the stakes.

"Ms Frost, I ought to tell you this isn't just some routine inquiry into stolen property, this is a murder investigation."

She sat upright when I told her this.

"The person who's said to have contacted you was shot and killed Monday last. Maybe you saw something about it in yesterday's papers. Two men shot dead in Bayswater?"

I raised my eyebrows as if to ask her a question.

"I think I saw something about it, yes."

"One of the two victims was the one who made the claim he'd got in touch with you. As I said earlier, he was a petty crook and it was him who stole your car. That's not in doubt. But he was adamant he'd got hold of something valuable he was looking to unload for cash, and we think that whatever he took from your car is what got him killed. So, if you have information pertinent to Police inquiries and are withholding it, we're talking obstruction of justice here."

She had poise; I had to give her that. She considered what I'd said for about ten seconds.

"A murder inquiry," she retorted.

"Yes. Two dead bodies and, so far, no official suspects." I refrained from telling her that, according to me, there was an unofficial suspect. "As I mentioned, we believe the deaths are connected to what Louis Phipps stole from your car, which is why I'm asking you to think carefully about what it was you say you haven't lost."

I realised my tone had become more serious as I spoke. I hoped I hadn't sounded too threatening, though, frankly, I wasn't bothered if I was.

"I can only stand by what I said, DS McGraw." She crossed her legs and looked straight at me.

"Were you aware your car was targeted for theft?"

"Huh?"

"Your car being stolen wasn't just a random theft and you the unlucky victim. Your car was singled out, and I believe what was inside was the reason for its being taken."

"My car deliberately stolen? Probably because it's a new car."

"No, there were other newer, more valuable cars near to where yours was. Your car was fingered by someone who wanted what was in it and he got the guy I mentioned earlier to take it for him. He took something from the vehicle and told the thief to dump it, but he chose to get in touch with you and offer it back to you. This makes it a step up from routine car theft because, ultimately, I believe it led to someone being shot dead. Why, at present I don't know; which is why I'm asking about what you lost."

"I don't know whether my car was targeted for theft or not, I'm doubtful that it was, but if it was, all I lost were some worthless party papers. That's it."

"It also makes me wonder why a DCI got involved in questioning the suspect. Car theft isn't usually what they deal with. Also, why was the car fingerprinted? That's not usual procedure for car theft either. You see where I'm going with this?"

"Frankly, no I can't, and I don't really think there's much more to say, is there? I've lost nothing of value and I'm glad my car was returned undamaged. Other than that I don't see how I can help you any further." She stood. I was right. They *were* great legs. I also stood up.

She walked back to her desk, sat down and picked up her phone.

"Was there anything else?" I took that as a sign I was being dismissed from her presence.

I was wondering whether to ask her if she knew someone named Richard Rhodes just to see her response as, at least on this point, if she'd said no, I'd know she was lying as I saw her getting out of a taxi with him late last night. For the moment I decided not to.

"No, I don't think so, for the moment anyway. Thanks."

She didn't reply and was talking into her Blackberry as I left her office.

Back at my desk I made notes about what I'd done that day. I included my visit to Simeon Adaka and his passing on to me what Louis Phipps had given him to hold on to. I also went into my visit to and conversation with Debbie Frost and my suspicion she was being less than truthful with me, though for the moment I had no proof of this. I omitted meeting with Richard Clements as it wouldn't do for Smitherman to realise that, after our previous enmity as students, a kind of friendship was beginning to evolve. If Smitherman ever thought I was priming his son-in-law for information, he'd have me transferred back to directing traffic wearing a tall blue helmet.

I thought about what Debbie Frost had said. She was adamant she'd lost nothing of value when Louis and Paulie Phipps had stolen her car. If so, why was Louis so sure he had something that the owner would want back and be prepared to pay considerably for the return of? Given who the victim was, it also raised the worrying issue that someone had to have told Louis Phipps that what was contained in the bag was in fact valuable. Was this just another crook like Phipps or, given what Debbie Frost did for a living, was there a political connection here?

She worked for a major political party in an exalted backroom position. She would have access to the thinking of the party at top level and its likely policy directions. She would know leading political figures, probably from all the major parties, as well as have contacts with a number of leading political writers on the main broadsheet newspapers. Louis Phipps, I was prepared to bet, wouldn't know a political principle if one stood on his foot. Yet Louis was sure he had something of value from the car owner and had, according to him, as vouchsafed by Simeon, attempted to make contact with Debbie Frost and been rebuffed. She denied any contact was made. Who might have told him this?

I phoned Conservative Party Headquarters and asked to be connected to whoever was Head of Research. I was put through to a Mr Paul Drury, who identified himself as acting head of policy research in the absence of the actual office holder who was away on long term sick leave. I identified myself as a police officer and said I was following up the case of the stolen car belonging to one of his assistants,

Debbie Frost. He said he knew about the theft a few months ago and, so far as he knew, she had since had the car returned to her almost intact. I agreed she had. I then asked about what had been taken from her car.

"She didn't take anything when she left here. She wouldn't have had any work materials with her anyway that day, given where she was going."

"Where was that, if you don't mind my asking?"

"A private family thing. She asked me to keep it quiet and I said I would. If she wishes you to know, she'll tell you herself."

After our conversations over the past two days, I doubted she'd even give me a scare if she was a ghost so I let it slide.

"So you didn't lose any party materials, anything like that?"

"No, I'm happy to say. Most people here take work files and their office laptops home occasionally for when they work at home but, happily, that hadn't happened here. As I said she'd not have taken anything work related with her where she was going."

"Not even old files that were of no use. Discarded papers, anything like that?"

"No. I wouldn't have thought so."

I requested he kept our conversation to himself and he agreed he would do that.

This was interesting. Debbie had said that her boss had assured her that what was in the bags taken was just stuff to be discarded, yet her boss was now saying that she took nothing with her. But she herself had admitted an official briefcase had been taken, as well as her handbag. Somebody was not being honest here.

I also got to thinking why a DCI would be involved in the questioning of a car thief. This was simply routine criminal activity by a practising criminal. True, it was a valuable car but if, as she'd said, she lost nothing of any value, why the involvement of a senior officer? I dialled West End Central and asked to speak to DCI Tomkinson. He was out of the office and I left a message asking him to return my call at his earliest convenience.

Rudolf had also said something about their house being searched by someone he regarded as *heavy*. Who was this person and what would he have been looking for?

The Branch office was occupied by a number of other detectives so I relocated to a small interview room along the corridor. I sat at the desk and opened up the envelope I'd obtained by using duress on a reluctant Simeon Adaka. I laid the contents on my desk. There were a number of printed sheets of A4 paper and several photographs. I separated the contents into two piles.

There were twenty-five sheets of paper and fifteen photographs. The pictures were well developed black and white and consisted largely of men in what appeared to be Khaki army uniform.

In the first picture two groups of about forty men were marching in formation across what looked like a parade square. In two others the soldiers were standing to attention whilst being addressed by an officer standing on a raised dais, with one picture taken from the dais behind the officer speaking, and another from the back of the group facing the platform. Three other pictures were of the soldiers engaging in assault course activities; climbing over obstacles of varying heights, or engaging in weapons practice. They were shooting at bull's-eyes a considerable distance away which had faces taking up a large amount of the surface area of the target, though I couldn't make out who they were. The remaining shots were taken inside what looked like barracks, with men sitting at tables either playing cards or socialising with a few drinks.

I was intrigued by one of the pictures. It showed what appeared to be a regimental badge, with a coat of arms across what looked like a bunch of red roses, all superimposed over a machine gun, with the words *Auspicium Melioris Aevi* in an arc beneath. I suspected this was a Latin term but I didn't know what it meant.

I looked at the picture of the officer addressing the squad from the dais. I didn't recognise the speaker but he looked stern and militaristic, dressed in what I took to be the uniform of an officer. He looked remarkably young to be an officer as, from the picture, I guessed he was no older than mid-twenties. The men listening were a cross section of ages, ranging from twenty to fifty, but they were all listening attentively as they took in whatever this man was saying. I looked at the other pictures but couldn't identify anyone from them. One picture showed a blindfolded man standing against a wall with a line of four soldiers pointing rifles at him, with the statement "*The fate awaiting traitors*" above.

Several of the papers contained photocopied articles from daily and Sunday newspapers with the dates ranging between early to mid-nineteen seventies. The headlines focused largely upon the deteriorating political and economic situation the country was facing, with the incidence of strikes increasing and chaos in factories and other workplaces across the country. Some of the articles looked very long. One piece in the *Sunday Telegraph* carried a banner headline asking the question "*Is the aim Communism?*", with an accompanying article stating that, in the view of the paper, all the current industrial strife caused by militant trades unions was designed to further the political agenda of the far left and the Communist Party, of whom many industrial organisers and union leaders were either members or supporters. The Labour Government was being accused of lacking the will and the gumption to stand up to what the paper referred to as industrial wreckers and tinpot despots with anti-democratic aims, drawing the conclusion that they didn't do so because they supported what the unions were doing.

One sheet had a list under the heading of "*Strategic*

Locations", which included power stations, mainline railway stations, Government ministries, telecommunications sites and Buckingham Palace. What was *that* all about?

But my attention was drawn to a two-page densely typed statement headed *"Manifesto"*. I began to read what it contained. In essence it was a call to arms. It said:

> *The time has come for all those who care for the future direction of the United Kingdom to stand up and be counted. No more Kowtowing to militant union leaders who want to hold the country to ransom with excessive pay demands, causing a sharp deterioration in the Balance of Payments and causing turmoil in the money markets. No more weak and spineless Government standing aside and refusing to take those actions required to put the country back on an even keel again. It's time for Government to Govern. If they can't, or won't, they should stand aside.*

I remembered the course I'd taken at King's about Britain in the 1970s. I'd learned that it had been a heady time of industrial unrest and bitter social divisions between the classes, with the breaking down of the consensus between management and workers and between the classes. There were strikes involving essential services on a regular basis and frequent walkouts in major industries. In 1974 the miners had gone on strike and this had even precipitated a General Election. The country had changed very considerably since those times.

I continued reading. The essence of the remainder of the manifesto outlined what the author believed the country needed, such as the reimposition of law and order and greater powers for the police to use force and break up strikes if the national interest was at stake. There was also a call for the police to be armed when dealing with situations such as the violent disorder that had occurred at the gates of the Saltley coking depot in 1972, during picketing by the miners' union, where so many miners and other sympathisers had amassed to stop lorries entering or leaving the depot that senior management, on police advice, ordered the closure of the gates so that potential mass civil disorder could be averted. This decision was felt by the author to be a turning point in industrial relations as the sheer numbers involved had overwhelmed the police to such an extent that, it said, *normal law and order had broken down and the power of the mob held sway.* The writer was adamant that a line had been crossed and *that ordinary law-abiding patriots could no longer stand by and watch the country they loved being overrun by Communist backed trade unions, some of whose leaders felt themselves to be more powerful than the Prime Minister and the Government.*

I'd heard all this before from my grandfather, who was as right wing as they came and all in favour of shooting strikers, and from what I'd read this was standard right-wing fare.

What caught my eye, however, further down the page, was the heading *"Recommendations"*. The writer had listed a number of things he felt should happen. I was surprised to read that he was advocating the formation of a private army to organise and mobilise to counter the impact of strikes that were, in the writer's view, increasingly contrary to the national interest. His argument was that a small group of heavily armed and well trained, motivated patriotic men acting out of a love of Queen and Country, could take over and run power stations and keep essential services operating. But what really surprised me was the next paragraph, arguing for an armed insurrection against the Labour Government of the time, stating that the use of force to overthrow this *lamentable and discredited Government* was justifiable as, not only was this body pursuing anti-democratic aims, it did not even have a popular mandate for what it was doing as, although the General Election in October 1974 had produced a Labour majority, the number was sufficiently small for the new Government to have to rule precariously.

He claimed to have the tacit support of leading figures in the senior ranks of the armed services, which would not intervene to attempt to quash any insurrection against the Government if ordered to do so, as well in the Establishment generally, such as financiers and editors of certain national newspapers, who would publish patriotic articles denouncing Communists in the Government and supporting the restoration of traditional British values of moderation and fair play. He also claimed to have heard, from a well-placed source, that the Conservative party, whilst not overtly supportive of any idea about what was a military coup in all but name, would not be too aggrieved at the downfall of industrial militancy brought about by patriots acting out of a sense of duty to protect their beloved nation.

The author also claimed to have a source inside Buckingham Palace stating that the Royal Family would not be displeased to see the removal of militant extremism at the top of political and industrial life. The source simply wanted to know when such action was to occur so the Queen and her retinue could be away from London at the time so as not to be implicated in any way.

I paused for reflection. I remembered hearing, during the course at King's, that there had been whispered talk about a possible coup led by disaffected military types who despaired of the direction the country was moving in, and for a while there were media articles discussing the likelihood of a *coup d' état*. But despite all the rhetoric and the anguished comments, however, the innate good sense of the British took over and such talk soon disappeared from the newspapers.

Had I not seen the pictures alongside this article I would have been tempted to think these were just the ramblings of some old military cove, sufficiently removed from the epicentre of power and simply expressing frustration at events he felt powerless to do anything about. But there was a worrying suggestion to some of the pictures. The officer addressing the ranks had the gleaming eyes of a zealot preaching to the converted. Those being addressed were also in uniform and holding rifles in the correct military position. There'd also been pictures of soldiers engaging in target practice, firing at bull's-eyes with large pictures across the centre. This didn't look like *Carry on Sergeant* to me.

I finished reading the recommendations. They were in a similar vein to what had already gone before, but my attention was riveted to the last one on the list, suggesting that the only effective and appropriate way to deal with those militants causing so much disruption to UK society was *Internment*, rounding them up and holding them in specially built *holding centres* and, for union leaders, especially anyone who was a communist, a death sentence, execution to be carried out by firing squad. I was amazed to see that, also marked out for an untimely demise, was the Prime Minister and other leading figures in the Labour Government, notably Tony Benn, who was despised with a passion on the right and seen as the architect and guiding spirit behind the left-wing militancy felt to be wrecking the nation. The more powerful trade union leaders, such as Jack Jones, Hugh Scanlon and Arthur Scargill, were also included amongst those to be liquidated.

The author then explained about contact he'd had with figures inside the Greek Military who, in 1974, had overthrown the democratic Government and imposed martial law on the country. He claimed to have offers of support from an unnamed general in the Greek army who was prepared to come to the UK to oversee the author's intentions and help put them into practice.

This was incendiary stuff and went far beyond any traditional right-wing invective that was popular at the time. Whilst paeans for greater law and order were not uncommon in most of the newspapers of the time, none were advocating the deaths of trade union leaders or senior politicians. Even extremist anti-immigration parties like the National Front were simply arguing for no further immigration to the UK and repatriation of those already here back to whatever country they came from. They weren't arguing for the extermination of immigrants.

I logged on to Google and typed in the legend, *Auspicium Melioris Aevi*, and requested a translation into plain English. It came back as "*Token of a better age*" and had some kind of connection to the *Order of St Michael and St George*. After reading through the blurb, it would appear that the group in these pictures had suborned this maxim for their own purposes as I couldn't see the connection between what this body represented and what was occurring in the pictures, and certainly not the sentiments expressed in the recommendations.

Was this what Louis Phipps had stumbled upon? Was this what he was assuming was going to make him rich? This would presuppose he knew who took the pictures, who the people in the pictures were and where they could be found now. Who would he know with this kind of information and how would someone like him come across such people? If the pictures had also been in the bags Phipps claimed to have stolen from Debbie Frost's car, what was her connection in all this? This also raised the question of why this material was in Debbie Frost's car. Why would she be holding onto them? Was she connected to one or more persons in these pictures? Did she know who these people were? Assuming Phipps was being truthful, why would she be in possession of such incendiary material? It was essential to find out who the people were in these pictures.

I looked at my watch and realised I'd been reading and examining pictures for more than an hour. It was now almost three and I could feel my guts rumbling. I poured a coffee and was thinking about lunch when DCI Tomkinson returned my call.

I thanked him and began by asking how he'd become involved in the investigation into the theft of Debbie Frost's car.

"I mean, with all respect, it's a routine car theft. I was just wondering what a DCI would be doing asking for fingerprints of the suspects in a case like this?"

"What was I doing? My job, that's what. Anyhow, why is this a Special Branch matter? As you rightly say, this was an ordinary car theft, no hint of espionage, so why do *you* need to know what I was doing?"

"I don't *need* to know," I tried to keep the ire from my voice. "But Louis Phipps was simply a small-time criminal. Stealing cars wasn't a new thing for him, or his brother. They'd been arrested for this before but they'd never had a DCI take an interest in their welfare. It's odd that a senior officer should get involved in this kind of case. I'm told you authorised fingerprinting, and my experience of car theft doesn't include routine fingerprinting. My interest is that the car was registered to someone who's a senior official in the Conservative Party, and there's a suggestion that blackmail was involved, so I wanted to know more about the suspect in case there was a wider agenda."

"And have you found one?"

"As of yet, no. The suspect, Louis Phipps, was shot dead last Monday night so I can't get anything from him. I'm also surprised MI5 was in on the interview. I'd like to know what this was all about."

"Sir," he instantly shot back. That was me put in my place.

"Sir," I replied formally.

"That's better. Now, to answer your question briefly, Five were involved because, as you yourself said earlier, the victim in this instance was a senior official in the backroom staff of the governing political party, and there was concern about what might have been lost. And, as you well know, Five don't get involved in day-to-day policing matters, which is why I was asked to become involved. But, as things turned out, the car was recovered and nothing of any substance was lost."

"Does that imply something was actually taken from the car?"

"Apparently something was taken, according to the car owner, but only a case full of old papers that were destined for the scrapheap, so she wasn't overly concerned at not getting them back."

"And MI5 were okay with this situation?"

"There's been no follow-up I know of, so seemingly they were."

"If that's the case, sir," I continued, "Who rifled Louis Phipps' flat whilst he was awaiting trial?"

"I don't know," he came back instantly. "Who told you this?"

"The landlord where Phipps lived. He said some heavy guy, as he puts it, came and searched his flat from top to bottom. Sort of unusual for a routine car theft when the only thing taken was a bagful of old stuff nobody seems to want, isn't it?"

There was a pause for a few moments.

"I wasn't aware of any searching of premises but, given who the suspect was, it could quite likely have been one of his criminal friends. It was nobody official, I'm sure of that. That chap, Phipps, he's dead now, isn't he?" he said almost casually.

"Yes, shot dead last Monday night."

"And you were there, I'm led to believe. You saw it go down."

"I saw *them* go down," I said flippantly. "I just heard two quick-fire silencer type sounds and then both Phipps brothers hit the deck."

"DI Harrow said you didn't see anyone pull the trigger, though."

"That's correct, sir. There was nobody either of us could

see. It was also dark in the area where the shots came from. Perhaps it was someone from the insurance company getting back at Phipps for all the hassles he's caused them from stealing cars."

"Pardon?" He sounded bemused.

"Nothing, sir, just a poor joke. No, I didn't see anyone around at the time of the shootings."

"DI Harrow also says that, so far, they've been unable to identify who the gunman might be."

I resisted telling him that, so far as I was concerned, there was only one suspect – an American hitman who'd been present near the scene minutes earlier. I'd already raised this belief with Smitherman and, for the moment, didn't want this broadcast any wider.

"That's true."

"CID has canvassed all around the area where the shootings occurred but have turned up nothing of any substance. Nobody seems to have seen or heard anything. Anyway, that's why I was involved in the early part of the case. Does that answer your question?"

Actually it didn't. I didn't doubt what he said was right. I just doubted I'd been told the whole story. Did he even know the whole story? Something was troubling me and I didn't know what.

"For the moment, yes it does. Thanks for the cooperation, sir." I hung up.

So, MI5 had been involved in the questioning of Louis Phipps after his arrest. They'd be involved if there was a security aspect to the case. But Phipps had only stolen a car, and whilst it was owned by someone high up in the governing party, albeit behind the scenes, who'd claimed she'd lost nothing of any importance in the theft, it didn't make any sense to bring in the security boys, any more than it made sense that Phil Gant had been hired to go after and kill the Phipps brothers.

It all kept coming back to the issue of what Phipps said he'd taken that was going to make him a shedload of money. I'd been looking at photographs of men training in military fashion and had read a garbled manifesto making the case for insurrection against the then Labour Government. Could this be something to do with it?

I took a couple of the pictures to the photocopier and enlarged them. The soldier's faces still didn't register with me but I could now see the targets being shot at. One was a head and shoulder image of the Prime Minister, Harold Wilson. A few others I took to be union leaders or Cabinet members because I didn't recognise any of them, though I did recognise Tony Benn and Arthur Scargill.

Richard Rhodes has said that Phipps was blackmailing someone high up in Government, which was why Gant had been hired. Leaving aside my disbelief at the notion of Louis Phipps even knowing the names of anyone in Government and that he'd even have a clue as to how to engage in such a sophisticated act, I doubted that was the real reason. Could Phipps have known something about someone that was the main reason for his being dispatched to the afterlife by Gant?

I needed to know more about those pictures as they had to contain a clue as to what this situation was all about. I had to know who the people in these pictures were and, in particular, who'd written the manifesto I'd just read.

I went onto the Branch database and typed the words "political extremism, 1970s" into the search engine. A whole swathe of pictures and links to other sites came up. There was lots of information about trade unions and far-left groupings like the *International Marxist Group* and the *International Socialists*, who'd now become the *Socialist Workers Party*. These groups mainly attracted the student activists who disagreed with the Parliamentary process and wanted immediate change in the social order by revolution. But I was more concerned about right-wing extremist groups as the manifesto was clearly written by someone with this constituency in mind.

There were all kinds of right-wing groups. Mostly they had anti-immigration in common, though some were anti-Common Market, as the European Union was then known as, regarding it as a sell-out of Britain's imperial heritage and a betrayal of the UK's Commonwealth interests. There were splinter groups advocating White Supremacy, including one attempting to set up a KKK group in this country. And at the other end of the spectrum were the predictable smatterings of fascist groupings arguing against what it saw as the Zionist threat and the forthcoming takeover of the world by Wall Street and Jewish banking interests.

But there was nothing listed about private armies contemplating armed insurrection against the Government of the day. I typed "Private Armies 1970s" into the database but, aside from information about private security firms, nothing was listed. I uploaded the picture of the officer addressing the soldiers on the parade ground into the system and requested recognition of the speaker but drew a blank.

This was puzzling. Anyone proposing to oust the government in the UK by violent means would clearly be seen as a threat to public order, as well as to the nation, which would mean a security file being kept and their leaders placed under constant surveillance. British political culture had never experienced any kind of seismic changes, such as government being overthrown by armed means. In fact the British experience was that even hardened left wingers became very moderate once ensconced in the back of the ministerial limousine.

But there was no record to suggest any surveillance had occurred. How could it be that a body like this, boasting of its contacts with senior and influential figures inside the Establishment and training up, ready for its attempted putsch, had escaped surveillance?

Finding out who these people were was now a priority. I also needed to know more about how these documents ended up in the possession of Debbie Frost. I knew who to contact about the first thing.

George Selwood was a self-confessed ageing fascist. His proud boast was saying he was the son of a man who'd marched alongside Oswald Mosely's Blackshirts in the 1930s and who had been present at the siege of Cable Street in 1936. His father had been interned alongside Mosely himself at the outbreak of war under regulation 18b of the Defence of the Realm Act, which provided for the incarceration without trial of those whose continued liberty was felt to be detrimental to the war effort. Upon release he'd continued espousing the fascist creed and had raised his son according to the same principles and beliefs.

Selwood himself had an almost vitriolic hatred of Jews and was an unashamed holocaust denier, which had led to his dismissal from several positions, including the Civil Service. It was just as well he didn't know I was a Spurs fan, a team traditionally associated with Jews. He had left the army after being told his views were inappropriate for an officer in the Queen's army to hold. Following on from this, he'd also been denied a lectureship in Defence Studies at a leading London university after the students' union found out about his political views and mounted a vociferous campaign against his being appointed. He'd sued the university, arguing his right to employ had been denied on the grounds of his political beliefs, which he said was unlawful, but the court had thrown the case out. He blamed the verdict on Zionist and Masonic influences at the top of the Judiciary.

For my purposes, though, he was a font of knowledge about who was who on the extreme right of the political spectrum after having been actively involved for a large number of years. He'd been active in all the major right-wing causes of the last fifty years, including ceding independence to previous colonies and mass immigration to the UK, and he had gone to prison for four months after daubing swastikas on a synagogue wall in Hendon. He knew all the major figures on the extreme right and, despite now being in his early seventies, still had a razor sharp memory.

I'd first encountered him when he was arrested at an anti-Iraq war demonstration after throwing a small plastic bottle filled with urine at demonstrators. I was one of the arresting officers and had taken him to Cannon Row police station. He was ultimately bound over to keep the peace and told not to attend any more such demonstrations. Since then I'd followed his career as a professional right-wing agitator and had picked his brain on a couple of previous occasions in the early days of my Special Branch career. I was hoping to do so again.

He lived in a small flat in a hard-to-let council block in Elephant and Castle, living amongst, as he put it, "nigger junkies, welfare scroungers, black single mothers with bastard children sired by different fathers making no contribution to their kids' upkeep, and general riff-raff," whom he described as people with no reason to be alive. The flat was untidy and cluttered with memorabilia of a life lived at the political extreme. There was a framed picture of Hitler proudly displayed on the lounge wall over the settee. There were several books espousing extreme right-wing ideology, including one with the provocative title *Did six million really die?* plus a copy of *Mein Kampf*. I saw a copy of *Hitler's War* by David Irving, a prominent historian and holocaust denier who'd claimed in the book that Hitler had not known about the holocaust. I expected to see a swastika displayed though happily I didn't.

He let me into his flat after I'd identified myself. He remembered me from his arrest and led me into his surprisingly neat and tidy kitchen. He made tea and put some biscuits on the table.

"What can I do for you, Officer?"

He was extremely well spoken, maintaining the English language was our greatest gift to the civilised world and must be protected because it was under attack from philistines who changed it to suit a politically correct agenda. To meet him for the first time, seeing how well presented he was and hearing how well he spoke, you'd be forgiven for thinking he was a retired diplomat. You'd be very wrong. In his youth and throughout his active political life, he'd been a nasty piece of work. He had convictions for violence after attacking left-wing demonstrations and had written several highly inflammatory articles for extreme right-wing publications about how to solve what he saw as the *Jew Problem*. Despite his age there was nothing avuncular about him.

"How's your memory?" I began.

"It's good. Why?"

"I'd like you to look at some pictures and see if you recognise anyone. Can you do that?"

I took the pictures out of the padded envelope and laid them on the table.

"Recognise anyone in these pictures?"

He put his glasses on and picked one up. He looked carefully at it and shook his head.

"Don't know anyone there."

"What about this one? Recognise anyone here?" I handed him the picture of the officer addressing soldiers taken from the parade ground.

He looked at it and smiled knowingly.

"Where'd you get this from?"

"You know who that is speaking?"

"I do indeed." He smiled at me, revealing several discoloured teeth. "Oh, my good Lord, this brings back memories."

"Well?" I awaited his reply.

"I'm surprised you don't recognise the speaker. He's quite well known, you know."

"Who is it then?"

"The man on the platform is the Honourable Mr Christian Perkins."

I looked suitably vague and shrugged, as if to say 'Who?' George Selwood looked at me as though I were being an idiot. Maybe I was.

"Christian Perkins is a Tory MP, has been for years. You still sure you've not heard of him?"

I had. He'd been an MP since the 1987 election and had acquired a reputation as an outspoken critic of the European Union and immigration. Some of the speeches he'd given over the years had been notorious in their impact. He worshipped Enoch Powell and peppered his speeches with references to his hero at every opportunity. No wonder I'd not recognised him. The Perkins I knew was an over-weight man in his sixties with a beard and thick black-rimmed glasses. In this picture, the speaker was a young vibrant man in the very prime of life.

"This is really him?" I asked, looking at the picture again.

"Oh yes, there's no doubt about it. That's Perkins alright. Where'd you get these?"

"That's not important at the moment. What's the story behind these? This doesn't look like a scout camp jamboree."

He sipped his tea whilst considering what to tell me about the events in the pictures.

"It wasn't. This was serious stuff."

"When were these pictures taken?"

"Between 1974 and 1975. The hope was that the Conservatives would win the election and act against the unions and other wreckers, but Labour won the October election by a small majority. When that happened the training intensified as everyone knew what was going to happen."

"What training? I mean, what's going on here?"

"We were based at this old disused army camp to practise military manoeuvres and do some rifle practice. They trained us hard for quite some time."

"I've also got documents alongside these pictures," I interrupted him. "If I've understood correctly, this was some small private army being put together by a few Colonel Blimp types who didn't like what was happening at the time. Am I near the mark?"

"Oh, it was much more serious than that," he replied instantly, fixing me with a nasty glare. His face looked as though he'd bitten into something bitter. "Please don't patronise the brave men in the picture, Officer. These men here were training for something that, had it come off, would have changed the entire destiny of this country, and for the better."

"Pray tell." I gestured for him to continue.

He looked me up and down then sat back and folded his arms.

"Someone as young as you couldn't possibly comprehend the political situation as it was in the seventies," he said slowly and deliberately. "This country was going downhill fast. We were a laughing stock in the eyes of the world. Political impotence, Government led by a Communist, trade unions running the country, most of them adherents to the hammer and sickle. Inflation up in the twenties per cent, strikes all the time. If it wasn't dockers, it was car workers or the bloody miners. Sometimes there was more than one union striking at the same time in solidarity with their *comrades*." He spat the word out. "We even had to demean ourselves and go cap in hand to a Jew-run body like the IMF to be bailed out, did you know that?"

I said I did and I was aware of what the mid-seventies had been like.

"Probably read about it in some book, no doubt written by some leftie academic trying to convince anyone who wasn't there that the situation wasn't nearly as bad as was made out to be. Well, it was. Trust me, it was a dreadful time to be a patriot and an even worse time to be English. It was clear things couldn't go on as they were. Did you know people couldn't even bury their dead at one time because of a strike by council workers?" His voice rose as he said this.

I remembered my granddad telling me something similar and saying that conscription should be reintroduced for all the long-haired layabouts. But he'd not said it with as much vitriol as George Selwood had managed to incorporate into his words.

"So, certain people decided that if Government was incapable of taking action and getting the country out of the mess it was in, they'd do it for them."

"And that someone was Christian Perkins," I stated.

"Not just him. There were others like him. Perkins had just left the army, which is where I'd first come across him, as he wanted to enter public life. He was asked to help with setting up and training a squadron of men who were ready to go to war to rescue the country. In this picture," he held one up, "Perkins is explaining why it was essential that everyone works and trains as hard as they can because this was a deadly serious enterprise and prisoners were not going to be taken."

"What did he mean by that?"

"That they weren't playing games. This was to be a noble enterprise aimed at winning back our nation from Communist saboteurs and they were determined to win."

"Who else was involved in this? Perkins wasn't in overall charge, was he?"

"Good Lord, no," he snapped back. "Perkins was well down the pecking order. There were several people ahead of Perkins, mainly in the armed forces."

"In the armed forces?" I repeated. "Actual serving military personnel were helping out?"

"They most certainly were." The pride he took in that fact was evident in the way he sat upright and thrust out his chest. "Yes, I know; you're going to tell me they had a sworn duty to the Crown and what they were doing was tanta-mount to treason. But these officers were patriots, one and all. Men who'd fought in the Second World War, fought the Mau Mau in Kenya, given their blood and their lives for their country. Men who marched past the Cenotaph every Remembrance Sunday with tears in their eyes as they remembered their fallen comrades. These were men of the highest principle, committed to rescuing their country from the Communist threat."

"So they weren't just playing soldiers." I wanted to get him riled and angry.

"They were not," he snapped. "As I said, the mission to rescue the United Kingdom was a deadly serious one. These men were being trained for a very serious, almost sacred task, which was to rescue the country they all loved, and would die for, from the enemies of democracy."

"How were they recruited? You couldn't just place an advert saying you wanted men ready to take part in a putsch against a democratically elected Government, could you?" I smiled.

"Recruitment was easy." From his expression, my flippancy hadn't impressed him. "Do you know there were so many volunteers wanting to do this, people ended up being turned away? How were they recruited? Word gets around. People know people who know other people, you know how things work, and gradually a small army was assembled and got ready for active service."

"How small was small?"

"Probably no more than a couple of thousand in the front line, I'd guess. Though of course others were ready to pitch in and help out when the time came. Many people wanting to help never had to wear uniforms at all, you know."

"How much training did these people have?"

"A couple of months. Basic military training – how to use weapons, how to think like a soldier, act like a soldier, that kind of thing. They were also subject to military discipline. One man was shot because it was suspected he talked to the left-wing press and warned them about what was happening."

"You mean like this?" I showed him the photograph of a firing squad.

"Yes, just like that. This really happened, it wasn't posed for."

"Who was this man? What was his name?"

"I believe it was someone called Eric Biggins, I think that was his name."

"You think he deserved this?" I nodded at the picture.

"I didn't disagree, if that's what you're implying. Discipline is discipline, whatever army you're in."

"So the soldiers took it as serious as those at the top did?"

"Every last one of them." He said this with a proud inflection in his voice.

"They knew what the aims of this mission were," I stated.

"Oh, really, Officer. Of course they did. They'd volunteered for it." He sounded proud.

"So, who was in charge of this escapade?"

"It wasn't an escapade. It was deadly serious. Who was in charge? You'd be surprised if you knew some of the people involved in this proposed action." He touched his nose almost conspiratorially.

"Men who were determined to rid this country of the scourge of Communism once and for all."

"From the uniforms and weaponry, there must have been someone financing it. Revolution doesn't come cheap. That's what Che Guevara said. Was it the same people?"

"That I don't know. I know some of the people who were behind the scenes organising, but I'm afraid I know none of the money men."

"Do you know the names of any of these people?"

"Quite a few of them, but their identities will die with me, I'm afraid."

I believed him. There was no point pressing him on this. I moved on.

"What was the significance of *Auspicium Melioris Aevi*? Did I pronounce that right?"

"Close enough. Do you know what it means?"

"Isn't it something like 'token of a better age'?"

"Yes, it is. The connection is with the Order of St George. My father named me George after him, you know. As he's the patron saint of England, and we were proposing to herald in a new and most decidedly better age, it seemed appropriate to use it to show people we were patriots, not counter revolutionaries."

"We? You were involved in this?" I wasn't sure why I was surprised at hearing this.

"Yes, indeed." He gave a kind of salute. "I'm one of those soldiers in the picture. That's why I asked where you got them from."

He picked up the picture of men marching across a parade ground holding rifles across their shoulders.

"There. That's me." He pointed to a man who looked to be around thirty.

I took the picture. Now he'd pointed it out, I could see that the man in the picture was indeed a younger George Selwood.

"How did you get tied up in this group?"

"I found out about it from Christian Perkins and I volunteered, like any good patriot in my position would do."

I mused about what I'd heard. Any scepticism I thought I had about this venture when I first saw the pictures had been removed. They were serious. I hadn't known that George Selwood had been involved, though I suppose I shouldn't have been surprised.

"So, how was this going to work? You were just going to go along to Downing Street and ask the Prime Minister to stand down and hand over power to some small army led by patriots with a gleam in their eyes, were you?"

"You're being facetious, aren't you, Detective?" He was not amused. "It would have been nothing like that. The aim was to wait until there was some major degree of social dislocation caused by yet another major strike and then call on the

Prime Minister to take some kind of decisive action. There were to be trained men placed at key installations like power stations and communications centres to ensure that essential services could continue. If the Government refused to respond, the intent was to go to Parliament whilst it was in session, go to the floor of the House of Commons and announce that we were stepping in and taking over. The Prime Minister and his Cabinet would be taken prisoner and held under lock and key somewhere whilst we formed an interim Government. There was someone ready to step forward and be the nation's leader until such time as a new Prime Minister could be appointed."

"Appointed. No elections for a new one?"

"In the short term, no. Democracy would have been suspended until the situation returned to normal. Once it was viable to have elections again, then suffrage would return."

"You're talking martial law."

"Yes, quite probably."

"What would the army be doing in all this? Were the armed forces just going to sit back and let the Government be overthrown from within?"

"As I said earlier, you would be astonished if you knew just how much support this action had at the very top of the armed services. Trust me, they would not have interceded with the actions taken. If anything, they'd have stopped anyone trying to stop us. We'd also had assurances from several top editors that we'd be portrayed as heroes for attempting to uphold the British way of life. The Bank of England was going to act to calm the nerves of the money markets. If union sympathisers at power stations or anywhere else tried to prevent us carrying out our plans, they'd be arrested. We had people trained to take over their positions and keep the lights on and the trains moving and the telephones ringing."

"Was this going to involve bloodshed?"

"Hopefully not. The hope was the Prime Minister would see sense and step down when he realised the range of forces against him. Our leaders would then inform the Palace a new Government was going to be formed as soon as democratically possible but, until then, an interim leader would be in place."

"And what was going to happen to members of the Government who had been deposed?"

I was curious to see if the answer was the same as the one I'd read in the recommendations part of the manifesto.

"They'd probably have been placed under arrest and held somewhere. Same with militant trade union leaders. They'd have been rounded up and put into custody."

"No plans for summary executions? That's what the military did in Chile in 1973 when they threw out the Government they didn't like."

"This is England, you know. We don't do that kind of thing here." He looked horrified. "The plan called for keeping the populace on our side, and you can't do that when you're killing people."

"What, like Eric Biggins here?" I nodded towards the picture.

Selwood said nothing.

"You think the people would have supported your actions?"

"Yes, I think they would," he said carefully after thinking for a few seconds. "Once they knew what we were doing and why, they'd have been fully behind us. But to be perfectly honest, though, I rather suspect most of them wouldn't care either way. So long as they have their new colour televisions and new cars and foreign holidays, most of the sheep out there aren't really that concerned with what's happening all around them. Look at the scum that lives around here; you really think they care about the heritage of this country? Our once proud nation is gradually becoming mongrelised. Damned miscegenation." He sounded angry and bitter.

"Sheep? You're supposed to have been doing this in their name. Isn't that a rather condescending attitude towards them?"

"Possibly. Possibly not," he said airily. "Actually it was being done *for* them, not in their name. They were going to be shown what strong leadership and decisive action could do. This country was not going to be allowed to go to the dogs."

"So, what happened? Why didn't the revolution take place?"

"That I never knew. We were all returned to units and the mission stood down. I did hear, though, that Mosley was too unwell to take the role offered to him. In the end we missed our moment and gradually, by 1976, the thing rather petered out."

"Mosley? As in Oswald?"

"Indeed. Perkins sounded him out but he was too ill by that time."

Mosley installed as Prime Minister? Perkins sounding him out? This was heady stuff.

"What surprises me is that there seemed to be no monitoring of this by the security services. I was looking for who this person was earlier," I nodded towards Christian Perkins' picture, "and I could find no evidence that security knew of the existence of this proposed action."

"Quite likely they didn't. I was told the secret services would not be too concerned if the Labour Government was swept away for the right reasons. So it's entirely possible a lid was kept on this situation. Many members of the security services were convinced the Labour Government of the time was a nest of Communists and would have enjoyed seeing them flushed away. You should read Peter Wright's book, *Spycatcher*. Tells you about his belief Labour were all commies. "

I thought about all I'd heard. George Selwood was not a person for small talk so I was sure what he'd told me was the truth. Mosley for Prime Minister. Is that what Phipps had discovered and was trying to blackmail about?

"So, there really was a plot to overthrow the Government in the mid-seventies?"

"Oh yes, there truly was. I wish it had happened and the swines had been thrown out on their ears, but in true British cock-up fashion, it never materialised. As a matter of interest, where did you find these pictures?"

"A long story. They came up in a case I'm investigating. I wanted to know if they were garbage or whether there was any substance to them. But you say there is."

He nodded. "Yes."

"Did you ever seriously believe this enterprise could be successful?"

"Certainly," he said confidently. "It was well planned, well funded and everyone knew exactly what was expected of them and was trained to do so. No, it would have been successful had it been put into practice."

"And the part in the manifesto calling for the execution of leading politicians and trade union leaders. That would have happened as well?"

"That wouldn't have occurred, Officer. Like I said, we're not a banana republic here. That wouldn't be our style at all."

It was now after six and I was back in the office writing up an account of my conversation and my impressions of what I'd learned so far. Before doing that, I entered the name Eric Biggins into the databank to see what was listed. An Eric Biggins, soldier of the Crown, had died early in 1975 after being accidentally shot whilst on a training exercise using 'live' ammunition. The usual words of condolences were expressed by an officer in his regiment. Such subterfuge could only occur if someone higher up was willing to cover it up. Selwood had been telling the truth.

I was beginning to reach the unpleasant conclusion that,

somehow, Louis Phipps had stumbled into the centre of something and been shot to keep him and his brother quiet. That would explain the presence of a ubiquitous element like Gant. But who'd hired him?

My musing was curtailed by the phone. It was Mullins calling from West End Central.

"You heard?"

"Heard what?"

"We're just going down to Brixton. Someone's been found dead. You were asking about that case with Louis Phipps the other day, weren't you?"

I agreed that I had been.

"We've just been informed that the victim in this case was someone called Simeon Adaka. He's listed as a friend of Louis Phipps. You know him?"

"I know of him certainly. What's happened?"

"We've only just had the tip. He's been found dead at home."

Holy shit. "I'm on my way."

Using the siren to clear the way, I reached Brixton remarkably quickly. When I pulled up outside Simeon's house, I saw a number of police cars with flashing lights and a pair of uniforms keeping the onlookers back whilst two others unravelled scene of crime tape to attach to the fence. I showed my ID to the constable at the door and entered.

I went along to the main front room where I'd spoken to Simeon only yesterday. Someone was taking pictures of the crime scene and a man with a white coat was writing something on a notepad. A man I assumed was in charge of the crime scene saw me, came over and identified himself as DI Pierce. He asked me who I was.

"DS McGraw, Special Branch. I'm told that Simeon Adaka has been found dead. He had information about a case I'm investigating."

"Adaka was a known drug dealer. I'm surprised the Branch had any use for him."

"What's the situation here?"

"From what I can gather, the deceased came back with his girlfriend and found someone searching this room. Place was all torn up so we're assuming he was searching for something. He appears to have got into a fight with whoever he found and, from the look of him, came off a poor second. Beaten to death he was. Body's right there." He nodded down.

I saw a lump on the floor covered by a white sheet. I knelt down and pulled back a corner of the sheet. It was indeed Simeon Adaka and he showed all the signs of having been on the receiving end of a vicious beating. His nose was broken, his lips were swollen and his left eye was heavily bruised and completely shut. He looked like the victim of a car crash.

"Someone clearly didn't like whatever drugs this guy was selling, eh?" another officer laughed. Pierce fixed him a stare and the man shut up.

"Do you know what whoever did this might have been looking for? Place is a tip and we haven't yet ascertained what, if anything's, been taken."

I did know but for the moment did not share that information.

"No, I don't. I know he was a drug dealer. Perhaps it was connected to that."

"You see his face? That's a little more than looking for a few spliffs. No, that was personal. Whoever did that was looking for something which I think they didn't find, which is why they did a number on the victim."

"Any ideas on who did this?" I asked.

"Uniforms are out canvassing and asking questions but I've no results yet. Whoever did it seems to have got clean away for the moment. I don't suppose we'll get much help from the people round here though." He said this almost dismissively.

I looked down at the forlorn shape of Simeon Adaka. He'd come home at the wrong time and found someone in the room and, as a result, was now dead. He was only involved because Louis Phipps had given him something to hold onto that he was convinced was valuable, and the fact that someone had beaten him to death convinced me it was valuable. What had Louis Phipps got himself involved in?

"Did the girlfriend see who did this?" I asked.

"She heard the victim call out to someone. He ran into the room and she heard a struggle. She got her mobile and called 999 and then, as she was calling us, some big bloke rushes past her, bumping into her and knocking her against the wall. She's got a nasty lump on her forehead but she's physically alright apart from that."

"She didn't see a face, I'm assuming."

"No. Just said it was a big bloke. She only saw his back."

I thanked DI Pierce and asked to be appraised of the situation as it developed. He agreed.

Back to the office. As I drove through the early evening traffic I considered a few points. Simeon Adaka had died a nasty death because he couldn't give up what he'd passed up to me. Phipps had stolen this package from a car owned by Debbie Frost. Last night I'd seen her in the company of Richard Rhodes. He was a big guy and I didn't doubt he was capable of doing what had been done to Adaka. I could connect those two together. She knew him. He knew Gant. Could she have been involved in the hiring of him to kill the Phippses? Where to find Rhodes now?

I contacted a friend I knew in the Drugs Squad and asked for any information on visiting Colombian drug lords as Rhodes had said he was working as a bodyguard for one. Such people would be routinely monitored whilst in London so I knew a watch would be kept on whoever it was. He came back and told me the only one known to be in London at present was Ruis leCuellio, currently visiting from Bogata and staying at a hotel in Knightsbridge. I thanked him and hung up after promising him a beer for his help at some point.

Finding leCuellio would mean finding Rhodes walking behind him. I phoned the hotel and found that the man concerned was still in residence. I drove to the hotel. At reception I was told that Señor leCuellio and his entourage had gone out for the evening to see a show in the West End but he didn't know which one or what time they were expected back.

In the corner of the massive lounge bar I spotted someone who I just knew was a police officer. Stake-out duty means having to wait around, often for some considerable time, and it produces a look of glazed monotony in the eyes, which radiates the impression of being interested whilst being bored rigid at the same time. I could spot the look a hundred yards away. It's the police version of the thousand yard stare. This man had it. He was killing time idly flicking through a newspaper and glancing at a television screen. I sat opposite him.

"So what time you on duty till?"

"Who might you be?" He asked.

I identified myself and the reason I was there.

"Sergeant Bales, Drugs Squad. LeCeullio and his gang have gone to see something at the National. Fucking drug dealing scum. The money they get from selling their filth, they wear leather shoes for the first time in their lives and stay in places like this. Bastards. You know how much a suite costs in this place? My whole fucking pension would just about get me a suite here for a week."

"They being tailed?"

"Yeah. There's someone behind them. He'll come back here then I go off duty."

"When they left, was there a big English guy with them?"

"What, Rhodesie? Usually he's with them but not tonight. As it's a cultural evening they've not taken him with them. I thought the only culture these fucking dagos ever encountered was put in the poisoned crap they sell."

"You obviously know Rhodes. Has he been with leCuellio all today?"

"Far as I know that's where he's been."

I stood up. "Rhodes comes back here, call me." I gave him my mobile number.

"Sure thing."

I left him to his boredom.

I was on the Branch database again, this time looking up all the details pertaining to Christian Perkins. There was a lot to read. Every actual or intending Member of Parliament has a file kept on them by MI5, which goes into considerable detail about their political beliefs and also their past lives. Friendship patterns, employment, countries visited, criminal record, known sexual perversions if any, written works in the public domain, plus details of any issues that person might be an expert in or keen upon. Is this person likely to vote for removing nuclear weapons from British soil? Is he/she a known racist? This helps the intelligence service when compiling a briefing for certain ministers who're considering appointments that might be security sensitive and involving access to secret documents. Any doubt is usually resolved by the MP concerned being denied the clearance to take the post in question.

Christian Perkins certainly had a chequered political history. He was now 66 and had been a Tory MP since the 1987 General Election. Despite the Tories being in power for the next decade, Perkins had never been offered any kind of ministerial position in Government. He had been a businessman since leaving the army, running a firm importing fine wines into the country from Australia and the United States amongst other places, which he placed with a range of top hotels. He still had a controlling interest in the firm but it was now largely under the control of his family.

He'd joined the army straight from university and reached the rank of staff sergeant but had decided not to extend his commission further once his time was up. I paused at that point. This was interesting. If this timeline was correct he was still a serving soldier when he was photographed talking to volunteers like George Selwood about armed insurrection and taking over the country.

Wasn't this treason? Didn't the oath a soldier swears upon enlisting have bound that person to serve the Crown in the form of Her Majesty's Government? As far as I could recall, the soldier's Oath of Allegiance did not specifically mention Government but the Constitution of the United Kingdom, such as it was, referred to the Crown in Parliament. If what I'd read wasn't treason, it was quite probably sedition at least.

Whatever, this was one for the lawyers. What I'd found was that Perkins had been a serving soldier at the time he was making speeches about overthrowing the established order in the form of the Labour Government. I wondered who else knew about this. But there was no reference on his security files to indicate there'd been any awareness of this activity. How was that possible? How could a private army of over a couple of thousand buy weapons and train to use them in pursuit of anti-democratic aims and yet MI5 get no hint of this?

I continued reading. He was assiduous in his pursuit of right wing ideology and was a member of several bodies aimed at influencing the Conservative Party to continue moving in that direction, such as *Clear Blue Water*. He was also influential in speaking out against what he continued to perceive as the underlying left-wing menace the country still faced and was a frequent guest of Conservative student groups at universities across the country.

There were several pictures of Perkins taken at events where he was either a speaker or attending as a delegate, with most showing him smiling benignly whilst shaking hands with young admirers or else in full oratorical flow. But my attention was caught by a picture taken at an election rally in 1992. Perkins was standing amidst a group of young people wearing blue rosettes and holding election literature. Standing two away from him was a smiling young woman in blue jeans and a cream coloured jacket. Debbie Frost. Her hair was still jet black and was up in a bun. She looked like a teenage girl about to blossom into the beautiful woman she now was. The radiant smile was still there as was the hint of mischief in the eyes. There were several other pictures of the group, including one of Perkins and Frost standing next to each other.

I could now connect her to Christian Perkins. That she knew him was undeniable but was this just a young politically ambitious student networking alongside an influential figure in the party or had she connected with him on another level? I cross-referenced her name against his. Over the past seven years they'd both been present at several annual party conferences and had been at the same fringe meetings. Nothing strange about this; she worked for the party and he was an MP. But they'd also been present at a number of weekend seminars organised by party sympathisers. They'd also been part of the same team that had been on a fact finding mission to Bulgaria when the possibility of increased trade with what was previously an Iron Curtain country was being considered as Bulgaria was in line to become a member state of the European Union in 2014. Over a seven-year period I could put them together at a number of different events.

I had photographic evidence of him speaking to soldiers and the testimony of George Selwood that Perkins was involved in a seditious plot against the then Government of the day. Louis Phipps had been in possession of these photographs and he'd taken them from a car owned by Debbie Frost. Did this imply a greater connection between the two? If I were to confront her again, would she deny any friendship between herself and Perkins? Would he do likewise if I asked him about her?

As things stood I didn't want to confront Perkins just yet. I had no real evidence other than the pictures, which I'd no doubt he could eloquently explain away. The manifesto he would probably say he'd never seen before and knew nothing about. There'd been no signature attached. I didn't doubt either he'd deny sounding out Mosley.

My mobile rang. It was Sergeant Bales calling from the hotel.

"Rhodesie has just returned. From the look of him I think he's had a few as well."

"Is he with the Colombians?"

"No, he's with another man. Don't recognise this one. They're in the bar."

"I'm on my way. Don't let them leave the hotel."

Bales said he'd keep an eye out for them.

I reached the hotel quickly, taking the scenic route along Grosvenor Road, around Hyde Park Corner and along Knightsbridge. I parked in a no parking zone and entered the reception area.

I couldn't see Bales anywhere so I asked the woman at reception if she knew where a Detective Bales could be found.

"The sergeant is being attended to in the office." She sounded Canadian.

"Attended to?"

She called to a porter and asked him to take me to the manager's office. It was part of a suite of offices behind the reception area. Bales was sitting against a wall with his head tilted backwards and holding a white bloodied handkerchief under his nose to staunch the bleeding. His white shirt had bloodstains down the front, as did his tie. He saw me looking at him and stood up.

"Should I see the other guy?" I asked, trying not to smirk at his misfortune.

"The two blokes, Rhodesie and the other guy, went straight into the bar, had a drink and went to leave. I intercepted them, told them I was a police officer and, as I was getting my ID out, Rhodesie sucker punched me with one to the schnozzle. They both ran off."

His voice sounded metallic through a mouthful of handkerchief.

"Don't suppose you saw which way?"

"'Fraid not, I was too busy bleeding."

"You know who the other guy was?"

"No idea, but I heard them talking when they first arrived. Sounded like a yank."

"American? You're sure about that?"

"Yeah, pretty sure."

An American. Phil Gant?

I asked the manager to show me the CCTV footage for the lobby for the past hour. He had it replayed in the security officer's little room. I saw two men arriving, one wearing a military jacket and holding a black beret in his hand, the other more casually dressed. It was indeed Mr Gant, the man I'd met in the alley outside Mickey's bar Monday night. Unfortunately there was no sound recorded so I couldn't hear a conversation. Rhodes had told me he was friends with Gant. But I was looking for Rhodes because of my suspicion he was party to the killing of Simeon Adaka. If he'd been with Gant and could prove it, maybe that theory was out the window.

I needed to find Rhodes. This was now a routine assault investigation. I called it in to the incident room at Scotland Yard and asked for a lookout to be kept for a Richard Rhodes, wanted in connection with an assault occasioning actual bodily harm on a police officer. I gave a description and a warning to be vigilant approaching him as he was likely to be dangerous.

FIVE

Friday

THERE'D BEEN no sightings of Richard Rhodes overnight but at least his name was now in the system. It would mean he wouldn't be able to shadow Ruis leCuellio, so losing his cushy little sinecure making it safe for some Colombian bigwig to flood the streets of the capital with even more of his filth. As a drug dealer known to be connected to a large cartel back in Colombia he'd be under constant surveillance, so if Rhodes was dumb enough to show up behind him, he'd be arrested immediately.

I contacted West End Central and asked for Detective Bales. Despite his late night and his bop on the nose, he was at his desk. I enquired about his nose.

"Fine. Been hit on the nose before, smarts for a while but it's alright now. Wife thought the bruising around it made me look sexy."

"You still following the Colombians around today?"

"No one is. LeCuellio and his scumbags checked out at seven this morning and, as far as I could make out, are now on their way to Amsterdam, no doubt to negotiate the selling of more of their shit. Why aren't we allowed to kill people like that on sight?"

"Where they flying from?"

"I'm guessing Gatwick, that's where their taxi's heading for. They probably aren't flying Cheapo Airways either. Fucking scumbag's probably flying first class with champagne all the way. You know what the fucking bill was for him and his entourage at the hotel? It'd take me three fucking years to earn what he just paid for a few weeks there. We play by the rules, those bastards shit on the floor in front of us and we're expected to fucking walk in it and say thank you."

"Yeah. Life sucks, doesn't it? Thanks for the heads up." I left him to his bitterness.

Special Branch maintains a permanent presence at all major airports so the departure of Ruis leCuellio and his family would be noted and his destination passed onto Schiphol in Holland. But he wasn't my concern. I wanted to know where Rhodes was. But initially I decided it was time to add a little pep to Christian Perkins' day.

Before leaving I contacted DI Pierce. I identified myself as the Special Branch officer at the scene of Simeon Adaka's death yesterday and asked if any progress had been made.

"No one's been arrested, if that's what you mean. The girl-friend calmed down a bit and gave us a statement. Said they came back and Simeon heard someone moving about and making a noise in the main room, so he goes in and argues with the bloke there, then a fight breaks out. Like I said, she only saw the back of whoever killed Simeon. Supposed to have been a big bloke wearing some sort of military type jacket and a scarf covering half his head. She said she never got a look at his face."

"Does she have any idea what this guy might have been after?"

"Funnily enough, I thought to ask her that. We do *do* police work down south, you know," he said, somewhat sarcastically. "She said she doesn't know. I asked if it could be drugs related, as Adaka's known to be a dealer in the area. She thinks it might have been something to do with whatever Simeon was looking after for a friend of his."

"What was that?"

"Claimed not to know. The friend was someone called Louis Phipps. You know him?"

"I know Louis."

I decided not to tell Pierce about what Adaka had passed onto me just yet. It didn't seem like the right thing to do before I'd confronted Christian Perkins. I also decided not to share my suspicion as to who the likely assailant was as he was already being pursued as a result of bopping Bales on the nose.

"Well, I don't know if whoever killed Adaka found what he was looking for. Place was a shithole so it's hard to tell. What could Adaka be holding that someone'd kill him for?"

"I don't know," I lied. "Louis Phipps was just a weasel. From my knowledge of him, I can only assume it's drug related. Maybe it was money."

"Possible. Anyway, you think of anything, get back to me."

I agreed I would. I hoped I'd lied convincingly.

I contacted a friend who worked for the Borders Agency. He confirmed that Rius leCuellio and his family plus three others had flown from London Gatwick to Schiphol in Amsterdam that morning. He was to be trailed by Dutch police all the while he was there.

At least Rhodes was out of a job. I wondered whether he'd got the bonus he'd boasted about receiving. It would be quite something to discover he'd not declared his earnings for tax purposes. I wondered if a call to the Inland Revenue was in order?

I decided it was time to put my findings to Christian Perkins. I phoned his office and was told he was working at home that day prior to holding a surgery in his South West London constituency later. I asked for his address and, as it was just up the road, I walked to his flat.

He shared a second floor flat at the top end of Buckingham Gate, behind Wellington Barracks, which was close enough almost to look over the walls into the gardens of Buckingham Palace. I'd phoned ahead and he was waiting for me when I arrived. He led me into the main room which, from the window, afforded a view of the street and all the tourists milling around excitedly. He was smartly dressed, wearing a suit and a crisp blue and white striped shirt. I thought that a man with a stomach his size ought not to draw attention to it by wearing stripes but I was no fashion expert. He had a neat beard and was wearing the kind of glasses Hank Marvin had made popular in the early 1960s. He took off his jacket and offered me a coffee, which I accepted. He asked me to sit, waving at a chair by his desk. He sat in the swivel chair and closed his laptop.

"You didn't say why you wanted to see me," he began pleasantly enough.

"That's right, I didn't. I was interested in your opinion of these."

I took a few pictures from the A4 envelope I was holding. I put on his desk a photocopy of the picture of him addressing a group of soldiers.

"What do you make of this?"

He picked it up. His eyes narrowed as he examined the scene.

"It's something that's come into my possession whilst investigating the killing of two people last Monday and I was curious about what you thought."

Perkins continued looking at the picture. Was he thinking about how svelte he was back then or what it was like to be the leader of fighting men being primed for action? I hoped he was more concerned with how the picture came into my possession. He nodded.

"What about it?" he replied.

"Recognise anyone?"

"Am I being accused of something, DS McGraw? Should I have a lawyer present?" he asked after looking at the picture for a few more seconds.

"No, you're not accused of anything so far as I know. That *is* you in the picture, isn't it? I mean, if it's not, tell me."

"You know very well it's me." Was this a flash of petulance?

"Or, what about this one?" I placed a photocopied picture of soldiers firing at targets with pictures of leading politicians in the centre on top of the other one.

He stared hard, trying to make out whose faces were in the middle of the target.

"Or, the piece de résistance, this one."

I gave him the picture of the blindfolded soldier standing by a wall with soldiers taking aim.

He was looking at the pictures with the same kind of focused concentration a surgeon might employ whilst conducting major surgery. His eyes narrowed. With his beard and the way he looked over the top of his glasses, and his puffy cheeks, he reminded me of a badger. He continued staring at the pictures for a few more seconds, then took off his glasses, put them into a case and into the inside pocket of his suit jacket.

"So, what do you want me to say about these pictures?" He sat back in his chair, his hands knitted together across his ample girth.

"I'm reliably informed this was not an exercise. I'm told the man in this picture was shot by the other soldiers and, no doubt by sheer coincidence, someone answering to the same name as this man is listed as having died from gunshot wounds around the same time, though the official verdict was death as a result of a training exercise using 'live' bullets."

"The army is a hard place, Detective Sergeant. People get hurt and, sadly, sometimes, a fatality occurs."

He made it sound as though people catch colds occasionally and what's the big deal.

"You accept these pictures are genuine?"

"Oh, they're real, alright. This was simply a training exercise. They were taken in the mid nineteen seventies, if memory serves. I was a soldier then, you know."

"Yes, I know, but this wasn't regular army, was it? This was something completely different. You saying it wasn't?"

"What are you implying by that?"

"I'm implying nothing. What I'm simply saying is that what's in these pictures was nothing at all to do with your career as a regular soldier. This was part of something quite different, if my sources are to be believed."

He stared at me for a few moments.

"There's a lot more of those. But you know that already. I've just bought a few along to show you. You can see they're photocopies, the originals are locked away," I continued.

"These pictures are almost forty years old. Why the sudden concern with them?"

"First off, I've only just become aware of their existence. My interest in them is because I believe they hold a clue to why two people were murdered three nights back. One of the two had these pictures in his possession. The person concerned was not a political animal in any sense of the word but I'm told these pictures are part of a blackmail scheme he was involved in. Now ..." I paused, "I believe the person in question couldn't even spell blackmail, never mind engage in it, so I'm doubtful about that claim. I believe his being in possession of these pictures was the main reason why he was killed. So, as you're featured prominently in them, and I'm reliably informed you played a key part in what was going on here, I'm curious as to what was it about these snaps that's led to two deaths."

"And you think I can help with that?" His eyes opened wide, almost a look of childlike innocence.

"Can't you?"

He put the tips of his fingers together against his chin. He looked as though he was being told by his wife she wanted a divorce and he was working out the likely cost, politically and personally. He held that pose for about twenty seconds. A long time to stare at someone and think.

"Those pictures are quite irrelevant. The context is very different now; I don't possibly see what's to be gained from this." He sounded very pompous. I suspected pompous came easy to him.

"You were, what, mid-twenties in these pictures and outlining some grand plan to overthrow the Government.

The man being used for target practice, what was his role?"

"Overthrow the Government?" He grinned. "Is that what you've been told?"

He looked at me with the kind of expression a teacher might have for a student he'd once regarded as very promising but who'd just said something particularly stupid.

"You are singularly uninformed about events, Officer. All this," he nodded at the photocopies on the desk, "was a very long time ago and frankly nobody cares about it. I don't know what you've heard, or who you heard it from, but I can assure you you're well off the mark."

"Really?"

"Yes, really."

"Okay, fill me in. Tell me what the mark is. What's going on in those pictures?"

"This was simply a training exercise. The blindfolded soldier was simply part of a joke at the end of training. Soldiers letting off steam after a gruelling exercise. He'd dropped a rifle or something like that so, for a laugh, he was tied and bound and put against the wall and subjected to a mock-up execution. There was nothing untoward about that at all." Perkins sounded exasperated, as though I were a stubborn child. "He wasn't harmed in any way."

"That soldier, Eric Biggins, died around the same time from gunshot wounds."

"I've already explained the situation to you, Detective. I've nothing else to say. I'm very busy so, if you don't mind, I'm off to my constituency surgery and then there's a public meeting later on I'll be addressing. I don't believe this conversation is serving any useful purpose."

He stood up.

"Eric Biggins died around the same time from gunshot wounds," I repeated. "I was told by someone who was there it was an execution. Are you denying that?"

"Yes, I am, and I'm afraid I have neither the time nor the

inclination to discuss the bigger picture with you just now. So, if you'll excuse me ..." He walked to the door and opened it for me.

I wanted to stay put and ask more questions, but I suspected I'd get no further cooperation so I decided not to. I thanked him and assured him I'd be talking to him again, and soon. He did not look pleased to hear that. I took the pictures and left.

I walked back to the Yard. He'd used the phrase "the bigger picture". What *was* the bigger picture? I'd seen a picture of a soldier being shot, yet Perkins'd said there was a bigger picture. What was bigger than armed insurrection?

Back at my desk I went online to view the Branch's list of army personnel, both past and present, and looked up the details pertaining to Eric Biggins. He'd joined the army straight from school and had achieved the rank of corporal. He was from Lowestoft and described as a good, honest and hard-working soldier who was no problem to command. Commendable, but I was more concerned about the circumstances of his death.

Army records said he'd volunteered for a weekend night exercise somewhere in the West Country. The exact location was not given for 'security reasons'. At some point on Saturday evening, he'd been on the top of a ridge attempting to manoeuvre into position when an exchange of gunfire occurred at the bottom of the hill and, in the crossfire, a bullet had hit Corporal Eric Biggins in the chest, killing him instantly. His body had been taken back to barracks in Aldershot and, after the army command was satisfied as to the chain of occurrences producing the death of Eric Biggins and that no blame could be attached to the army, his body was released for burial by his family, and he'd been cremated with full military honours in his home town. The officer commanding the weekend exercise was Sergeant Christian Perkins. Perkins had also represented the army at the funeral.

Eric Biggins had not long been married at the time of his death. He'd married his childhood sweetheart, Lucy Grey, only eight months before and, when he'd died, she was almost three months pregnant. I exhaled reading that. It was sad knowing he had a child he never saw. I wondered if he even knew.

I phoned the number listed and discovered his wife still lived at the same address. She'd remarried and had a child by her new husband, Jack Hamilton, though this man was an engineer. I identified myself as military police calling from London and told her the reason for my call.

"It's nothing to worry about, Mrs Hamilton. It's just routine. Every so often past records are checked to ensure everything is as it should be, you know how institutions like the army work."

She agreed she did and was happy to answer questions.

"What were you told about Eric's death, Mrs Hamilton? Who told you?"

"A pair of officers came to the door, a man and a woman. They told me that Eric had been hurt in some accident at a training thing somewhere and had died. They assured me Eric hadn't suffered and would have died instantly. They were very comforting about it, promising me all the help I needed to get through the times ahead. I was very grateful for their help but I had my own family nearby, as well as Eric's. Eric came from a military family, you know. He'd wanted to follow in his father's footsteps, become an officer like him."

"What happened after that?" I asked.

"Oh, it's all a blur, really. I don't remember too much about it if I'm perfectly honest. I was just pregnant with my Roger at the time so I was trying not to get too worked up. I don't remember much between being told he was dead and his cremation. The man in charge of the exercise Eric'd died on came to the cremation service to represent his regiment, which was sweet of him."

"Can you remember who that was?"

"Yes, I can. It was a Sergeant Perkins. Funny, he's a Conservative MP now."

"Is he? I didn't know that," I lied. "One other thing. There was no suggestion of foul play, anything like that, was there?"

"No. The officers told me Eric's death was accidental and he was just in the wrong place. They didn't say anything about foul play. Everyone involved said it was a terrible accident and how sorry they all were it had happened. Nobody was to be charged. The brass accepted it was a tragic accident and it went down as that."

"Yup, that checks with the records here. I'm sorry to be bringing up matters from so long ago but bureaucracy needs feeding, so they say. The moment something like this isn't checked, it'll come back and bite us you-know-where." I heard her laugh.

"Eric's father had the matter looked into at the MOD, pulled a few strings here and there, but he was satisfied with what he heard about his son's death. It's just a shame Eric never knew he had a son. I named him Roger, which was Eric's middle name. He's almost 39 now and was the image of his dad when he was born. He's a soldier as well, a major. He's done what his dad was never able to do."

"Congratulations. Thanks once again." I hung up.

So there was no doubt about Eric Biggins dying. But George Selwood had said it was an execution whereas Perkins said the picture was just routine nonsense being played out by high-spirited soldiers. What had begun with my looking into why Phil Gant had killed the Phipps brothers was now spiralling into something quite puzzling. Louis Phipps had stumbled blindly into something he had no idea about and, through trying to sell back what he'd stolen, had got himself and his brother killed. Debbie Frost had denied any contact from Louis Phipps but, if that was the case, how did Gant end up on his trail and eliminating him? How would he even know about a pair of lowlifes like the Phipps brothers? Someone had to have pointed him in that direction.

My bet was that Debbie Frost was part of this equation. It had to be something in those pictures. Perkins had admitted it was him in one of them but denied anything inappropriate was occurring; just soldiers on exercises. What was the bigger picture he'd alluded to? Had George Selwood not been completely honest with me? As repulsive as his beliefs were, he was at least honest in what he believed in. If anyone was lying, I was certain it wasn't him.

Smitherman was at his desk talking to someone I didn't recognise when I knocked and entered his office. The man looked to be in his early fifties with immaculately groomed greying hair. He was impeccably dressed in what looked an expensive jacket with a coat of arms on the top pocket I was sure was the crest of his regiment. His tie had a smaller version of the same crest. His slacks were light coloured but had a razor sharp crease and his shoes were almost glowing. My shoes would have to be painted to look anything like that. There was an attaché case by the chair.

"The very man. We were just talking about you. Come on in."

I did.

The unknown man stood up as I entered. He stood almost to attention. I began thinking I might have to salute. We shook hands. His grip was very limp for a senior military man. Softened by too many years behind a desk?

"Take a seat." Smitherman gestured to a chair. I sat across at right angles to the unknown man.

"This is Colonel Peter Stimpson, who's attached to MI5. He and I were just talking about the case you're following up on."

"Can I ask what this case has to do with them?" I was puzzled.

"You may," Stimpson replied. Nice of him. "A colleague of mine, Colonel Warren, asked me to talk to DCI Smitherman about something he'd enquired about. I believe you were just talking to a Christian Perkins about the death of a soldier on a military exercise. Am I correct?"

"Yeah. I talked to Perkins a couple of hours ago. Didn't take him long to get on the blower, did it? How does my interviewing him about a Branch case impact on you?"

There must have been something in my tone and expression because Stimpson looked as though he'd bitten into something sour.

"Now, there's no need for such belligerence, Detective. I simply wish to know why it was you felt the need to question Mr Perkins about some pictures."

I looked at Smitherman. He nodded.

"A man I was bringing in for questioning on Monday last was shot dead whilst I was standing next to him. Nobody saw who did it, though I have my suspicions. CID is investigating and is treating it as murder and, so far as I know, there've been no arrests made."

Smitherman agreed there hadn't been. Stimpson nodded intently.

"I've uncovered a lead suggesting one of the victims was attempting to blackmail somebody in Government so I've been investigating that lead and, in the course of so doing, I came across a package of articles and photographs which, I'm told, related to an organisation in the mid 1970s plotting to overthrow the Government."

"I see," Stimpson nodded sagely. "And how does this involve Mr Perkins?"

"He's in some of the pictures."

Smitherman looked surprised. Stimpson didn't.

"He was," I reiterated. "He was dressed as an army officer addressing a group of uniformed soldiers on a parade ground, though official records suggests he never rose above sergeant. I believe the reason why Louis Phipps was shot and killed has to do with these pictures and I'm backtracking, trying to find out what's so special about them that they ended up getting someone shot."

"These pictures were owned by Mr Phipps?" Stimpson asked.

"No. They were found in a car he stole. I'm led to believe he attempted to sell them back to the car owner but that person's denied any contact being made. However, soon after contact was or wasn't made, Phipps was shot dead. Is that a coincidence? Phipps was just a street punk, as was his brother, but I think they were both assassinated to keep them quiet."

"Assassinated, eh?" Stimpson mused. "Do you know who killed these men, Detective?"

"I think I do but, so far the Branch isn't investigating that. I'm pursuing the blackmail angle."

"You're sure you know who killed these men?"

"I think so." I looked at Smitherman. He was non-committal.

"Any evidence of a blackmail plot?"

"None so far. Personally I don't believe the man concerned could organise a blackmail scam if his life depended upon it, and in this instance it did." I grinned. No one else did.

"Thus," I continued, "I'm wondering if there isn't another more sinister agenda involved. So, as he was identified in the pictures by one of my sources, it seemed logical to ask Perkins what the pictures were supposed to be about. That's why I went to talk to him."

"You say this person acquired the pictures from a stolen car. You know whose car?" Stimpson looked directly at me.

"Yes, I do. It's amazing what you can uncover doing routine police work, isn't it?"

Smitherman glared at me.

"And do these pictures belong to the car owner?" Stimpson ignored my sarcasm.

"Person says not. Claims not to have had anything of any value taken from the car at all. The same person admits to losing a bag but says it just had lots of stuff about to be junked, yet the victim maintains he took something that would be of considerable value to someone. The pictures of Perkins in uniform were amongst the things this guy took from the car."

"Who was it who had the car stolen?"

"Do I have to answer that?" I looked at Smitherman. "This is a Branch case."

Stimpson looked at me with a kind of "who do you think you are?" smirk.

"So who do you believe?" Smitherman quickly interjected.

"Louis Phipps had nothing to gain by bullshitting. He's not politically aware or motivated. He just saw a chance to make some money. I believe his story. I believe the person concerned is lying about what was lost when their car was stolen."

"Why do you think this person's lying, Detective?" Stimpson settled back into his chair.

"I think something's being covered up. That's what I'm looking into. I've spoken to two people who say Phipps contacted this person. One was even in the room when the call was made and claims he heard what was said. The pictures I showed Perkins were from the bag that Phipps stole from the car, yet this person denies losing anything. There has to be something there, otherwise why does Perkins go crying to you 'cause I've spoken to him about the pictures?"

I looked at Stimpson. He radiated the kind of smug arrogance that comes from working behind the scenes when your views and sources are secure from any kind of public scrutiny. I didn't like him and I didn't like his shiny shoes or his creased trousers.

"That's not quite what this is about, Detective. Christian

Perkins maintains close links with the intelligence community in this country and has done for quite some while."

"What, he's ex-MI5?"

"That need not concern you. Suffice it to say he has been useful to us in the past. We just wanted to know why a Special Branch detective went to his home and showed him pictures taken whilst he was still in uniform and implied he was part of some conspiracy to overthrow the British Government." He said this almost in a tone of disbelief.

"The wrong uniform, as well. He was never a major, yet in the picture he is. Anyway, that's what my source told me the people in the picture were engaged in."

"And who spun you this tale of intrigue, might I ask?"

I smiled at him and said nothing.

"Do you believe that's what the pictures are showing?"

"I'm just investigating at present. What I do know is that Christian Perkins never rose beyond being a sergeant but, in one of the pictures I've obtained, he was wearing the pips of a ranking officer on his shoulder." I paused. Stimpson continued staring at me. "In another picture a man's being shot. Perkins says the picture was high jinks but the man in the picture actually did die from gunshot wounds around that time."

Stimpson nodded sagely but said nothing.

"I came across these pictures whilst looking into why Louis Phipps was shot dead because he was supposed to be blackmailing someone. What I *do* believe is that Phipps wasn't blackmailing anyone. That's beyond his imagination. I believe he was silenced because of what these pictures mean to somebody. That's what makes it a Special Branch matter. Especially considering where the pictures were obtained from."

Stimpson tapped his fingers on his knees. Impatient or nervous? Or bored?

"In sum, Detective, do you believe you're anywhere near

to cracking the blackmail angle you say you're investigating?"

"Working on it, making progress. Even if you're stumbling, at least you're going forwards. That's what my old dad says."

He looked at me as if he'd not understood what I'd just said. Perhaps he hadn't.

Stimpson stood up and picked up his bag.

"Well, gentlemen, mustn't detain you any longer. I just popped by to put DCI Smitherman in the picture." He looked at me. "I'm sure he'll decide what it is you should be told at the right time."

He left the room after extending his limp hand again for me to shake.

"What did M want?" I nodded towards the door.

Smitherman sat still for a moment. He was thinking. Stimpson had clearly told him something important and the issue now was what I was to be told. If anything.

"You don't like Colonel Stimpson, do you?" Smitherman stated.

"Am I that transparent?" I grinned.

"Well, what he had to say was quite revealing. I'm not able to go into everything he said but his presence should have told you this case has security implications."

"Huh?" I was bemused.

"As I said, I can't tell you much more just at this moment. Let's just say that MI5 are aware of your suspicions about Mr Gant and why he may have been involved."

"What, they know he killed the Phippses? Why hasn't he been brought in?" I asked.

"It may not be that easy. I don't know the whole story but it does seem that, for the moment, Gant is in the clear."

I then spent the next five minutes explaining to Smitherman everything I'd been doing in the past few days – who I'd seen and what I'd heard, though again omitting any reference to picking Richard Clements' brain about Debbie Frost. I told him I'd got the information about the plot to overthrow the Government from a very reliable source and it was this person who'd identified Perkins for me and also told me about the central role he'd played in the plot.

"Yesterday," I continued, "the person who told me about what Phipps had found and his contact with Debbie Frost was found dead in his flat. Beaten to death. He caught someone rifling the flat and was attacked and died as a result. Whoever did it was looking for the package of stuff Phipps lifted from Debbie Frost's car. He didn't find it 'cause I had it. He'd given it to me earlier yesterday. The suspect is supposed to be a big guy, and I think I know who that might be. I saw a CCTV clip last night and this same person was with Gant. Also, the night before, I saw this same guy get out of a taxi with Debbie Frost and go into her flat, so she clearly knows a lot of people in this scenario."

"You're sure it was him?"

"Oh yeah. I didn't recognise him straightaway but he left the flat soon after and I saw him then. It was definitely him, no question. No mistaking a big bastard his size."

"So, why would she say she lost nothing?"

"That's what I'm going to go and ask her when I leave here."

Smitherman agreed that was a logical move.

Before that, though, I had to make a phone call.

George Selwood was still in his flat. He seldom went out, being a fully paid-up misanthrope, hating almost everything and everyone. If killing was legalised for people you disliked, numbers in his part of Elephant and Castle would diminish very rapidly. He encapsulated the fascist philosophy in its entirety, especially the deep rooted pessimism about humanity that all extreme right wingers I've ever encountered seem to possess.

He remembered me from our conversation yesterday. I

began by asking him if what he'd told me about the involvement of Christian Perkins was really true.

"Oh yes, there's no doubt. Mr Perkins was most definitely involved in what we were being trained for. I can guarantee you that."

Listening to him on the phone, if you didn't know who it was on the other end, you'd be forgiven for thinking you were conversing with someone in the very highest socio-economic class, rather than a self-confessed fascist who hated the human race. Or at least a very considerable percentage of it.

"I've spoken to Perkins. He's just shrugged it all off. Didn't seem to attach any importance to it at all. But, what I want to know is, the picture of the bloke blindfolded and about to be shot by a firing squad. Perkins maintains it was just a laugh, but you mentioned the name Eric Biggins. I've checked records and a soldier with that name died around the same time from gunshot wounds received on a training exercise. It's listed on army records as an accidental death."

"It was a training exercise but, trust me, there was nothing accidental about it. Perkins it was who gave the order to have the man bound and blindfolded and then shot."

"You're not bullshitting me, are you, George? Because if I find out you're lying, I'll put your name, address and your political history and beliefs on the websites of every left wing group I can find."

I tried to sound threatening but it didn't quite come off.

"I have no reason to lie to you, Officer. I don't have too much longer in this wretched world so I've nothing to lose at all. But I swear to you, on the word of Adolf Hitler, that what I've told you is the truth." He said this slowly and methodically, as though reading from a script.

This was hardly a ringing endorsement but I took his word to be the truth.

"There's something else as well. The four men in the

168

firing squad. Are there any still alive and, if so, do you know where they can be contacted?"

"I'm not sure. The only one I knew was someone called Rothery, but I don't know if he's still alive or where he lives."

"I'll check it out. Thanks for that. I appreciate the help."

"There really was a plot to bring down the Labour Government in the seventies, you know? You've seen the pictures. I've pointed out Perkins' role in it. He wrote the manifesto for it."

"Really? Perkins put that stuff together?"

"He did," Selwood stated firmly.

"Hmm, interesting. Thanks for the heads up."

"He was always a pompous ass, was Perkins, and I doubt he's any better as an MP, especially a *Conservative* MP." He practically spat the word out.

"I thought you'd be on their side," I said, almost light-heartedly.

"Oh, good God, no. They're just as responsible for the mongrelisation of this once great country as the Socialists who sit opposite them. All the immigration they've encouraged has done is to let the Third World move into this country and turn what was a once proud Christian nation into a black Muslim state. Are you aware mosques now outnumber Christian churches in this area? If we'd carried our plan through, this country wouldn't be what it is today, that I can assure you of."

I thanked him for his trouble and hung up.

I was back on army records, checking anyone with the surname of Rothery. Only one was listed. A man named Jonathan Rothery had joined the army in 1969 and left in 1983. He was still alive and listed as residing in Watford. If the records were correct, he'd be in his early sixties today.

There was a number listed for his address. I phoned and it was answered by a woman who said she was Rothery's daughter, Claire, and that her father lived with her as he was permanently in a wheelchair as a result of a car crash. Her mother had died some years ago and he lived with his daughter as he needed constant care and attention. Jonathan Rothery wasn't in as he was attending physiotherapy at the local hospital but would be home later. I thanked her and hung up. I arranged to go to visit him.

It was long past time for something to eat. I grabbed a sandwich from the café in St James's Park and sat on a bench to eat and take in the spring sunshine.

What had begun as two men taking refuge in the bar owned by a friend so as to hide from a man shooting at them was now developing into something quite unexpected. There seemed to be several different strands and I felt I knew nothing despite all the questions asked.

Since the Phipps had died, Simeon Adaka had met an unpleasant end because Louis Phipps had given him something to keep safe for him, and he'd maintained he'd obtained it from Debbie Frost's car. She was central to this case but I didn't know how or why. Time to add a touch of indigestion to her afternoon tea.

Before I left the office I phoned Mickey at his bar.

"You like politics, don't you? Fancy going to a political meeting later today?"

I told him what I'd like him to do.

I was back at Millbank, at the headquarters of the Conservative Party. I asked to speak to Debbie Frost and I was given a visitor's badge and escorted to her office. She was on her mobile when I entered, pacing around by the window. She looked at me as though I were a bad smell wafting into the room. She said she'd call back to whoever she was talking to.

"Now what?" She sounded exasperated. "I'm beginning to think you're stalking me."

"You should be so lucky." I grinned and sat down without being asked to do so.

"I'm guessing you want something else." She sat back in her Parker Knoll recliner. There was a jacket hanging on the back to remind everyone whose chair it was. She looked at the envelope I was holding quizzically, as though it contained exam results she was anxious to see.

"Actually no, I want the same thing as before, the right answers to my questions. I think you're lying to me, Ms Frost." I leaned against her desk.

She said nothing. She continued to stare at me. Richard Clements had said she was a looker and she was certainly that. I couldn't help my eyes lowering to take in a fleeting glimpse of the swell of her body beneath her blouse. I loved her hair and I already knew she had great legs. In another reality I could really fancy her. But not this time around.

The silence lasted for a few more seconds.

"Do I need a lawyer? Why are you on my case?" She was attempting to sound pleasant as she spoke but her distaste at my presence was apparent.

"Now, that sounds like a persecution complex to me. Why would you need a lawyer? I'm just asking questions in the course of an investigation where, since last Monday night, three men have been killed."

"Three? You told me two yesterday."

"That was before yesterday afternoon when a man known to the other two guys was brutally beaten, and he died from his injuries. The person who did this was looking for whatever it was that got stolen from your car. So, that makes three fatalities. All three knew each other, all three in on what was taken and knowing what it was, yet you still maintain nothing was stolen from you that was worth anything."

She looked sullen, like a teenage girl told her skirt was too short and she had to change before being allowed out the door for her date.

"I do. What else can I say?" she shrugged.

"Why were you parked at Waterloo station, Debbie? You

don't mind my being informal, do you? Was this for your job?"

"What I do takes me all across London, Detective. It's quite likely I was on party business. It was nearly four months back. I can't remember exactly. Besides, what's that got to do with anything?"

"As I believe I mentioned when we spoke recently, your car was targeted. It was stolen to order and I believe it's because somebody wanted what you were carrying. Therefore, somebody had to know you were going to be in the place where you were parked. That make sense?"

"I suppose so."

"Okay. So somebody had to arrange for your vehicle to be stolen. That would suggest somebody who's familiar with your movements on the day in question. Someone who would know where you were to be at the time your car was stolen. Yeah?"

"Okay." She shrugged.

"I think it's somebody who works in the same place as you, or is at least familiar with your movements. Was this a routine thing where you were? I mean, do you do it at the same time every week, every month, that kind of thing?"

"There are times when that occurs but this wasn't one of them."

"So, what does that suggest to you?"

"Doesn't suggest anything. All it suggests is my car was stolen but it was recovered. I'm afraid I don't buy into this theory you seem to have about my car and what I'm supposed to have lost."

I waited for a few moments. I looked around. Her office was all mod cons. Everything looked new and the room was well appointed, even if the view was only rooftops behind Millbank. The tops of buildings in Smith Square could be seen. There was a portrait of Margaret Thatcher on the wall behind her desk.

"You know what strikes me as odd in this case?"

I continued before she replied. "Phipps says he contacted you about what he took from the car. Not too much longer after that, he gets shot, so does his brother. The other man I mentioned just now? He was holding what Phipps had passed on to him, and he too gets killed, but he didn't die nicely, beaten to death actually. So, all three were connected. Funny that, wouldn't you say?"

"There's nothing funny about people dying, Detective. You're very flippant, aren't you?"

Time to raise the stakes. I took a picture from the A4 envelope I was holding and laid it on the desk in front of her.

"Recognise anyone in this picture?" I asked.

I'd given her the one of Perkins addressing the squad from the dais.

She looked closely at the picture. "No, I'm afraid I don't. What does this have to do with me?"

"You know Christian Perkins?"

"Of course I do. He's a senior MP in the party. I've worked with him on any number of occasions."

"That's Perkins on the dais talking to those soldiers."

She held the picture closer to her eyes and squinted.

"I wouldn't have recognised him from this. Anyway, he used to be in the army. So what?" She was starting to sound annoyed at my questioning her. Good.

"Perkins never rose above sergeant whilst in the army, but the man on the dais has the uniform of a ranking officer. Notice the pips on the shoulder?"

"And?" Her eyes opened wide. She ran her fingers through her hair. I wasn't certain if I liked her hair better than her legs. I decided I preferred her legs.

"Did you know your friend, Mr Perkins, Mr Law-and-Order, hanging's too good for the buggers, was actually involved in a plot to organise a coup against the Government in the mid 1970s?"

"Oh, that's preposterous, Detective. Christian involved in

something like that?" She sat back in her chair and shook her head.

"Does sound peculiar, doesn't it? But I have the testimony of someone who was there, who was part of the squad being trained for just such a move. There's a lot more pictures like this one. You want to see them?"

"Christian is a patriot. The very idea . . ." Her voice trailed off.

"Next time you see him, tell him you've seen this picture. Also," I took out the one of the blindfolded soldier and showed it to her. "Tell dear old Christian you've seen this one as well. Ask him if the name Eric Biggins means anything to him."

"Should it?"

"Yes, I think it should. The man in the picture there," I pointed at Biggins, "was shot dead by a firing squad. Perkins gave the order to shoot, killed the guy in cold blood. He even went to the man's funeral, can you believe that?"

She looked at me and said nothing. I wondered if she already knew all this. Would Perkins have told her? Was I boring her by stating what she already knew?

"Do you already know this? You don't seem surprised."

She looked out the window and shook her head.

"Ask him also what *Auspicium Melioris Aevi* means. He'll know what I mean."

"I went to a school that offered Latin. *I* know what it means."

"Even better." I stood up. "You can translate it for him. Oh yeah, before I forget, do you know someone named Richard Rhodes?"

She paused. "I'm not sure. I might do but can't place the name. Who's he? Is he another conspirator?" Was that a tone of levity in her voice?

"Doesn't matter." I looked at her then left the office. I resisted the temptation to sing *We'll meet again* as I did so.

I was on the Tube to Watford. It was now peak commuter time on a Friday afternoon and the carriage was crowded as far as Neasden, at which point I was able to get a seat.

Interesting that Debbie Frost had not admitted knowing Richard Rhodes. There's no mistaking a guy that size and I saw him and her getting out of a taxi last Wednesday evening. That clearly suggested she was lying. I wondered what their connection was. Were they friends or was their relationship, if that's what it was, a business one? Was she aware that his recent employment had been babysitting a Colombian drugs pusher around London? The Conservative Party was officially anti-drugs. What would it say about one of its top employees consorting with a mercenary soldier who also just happens to be helping to make drug deals in London possible? An interesting moral quandary, I was considering as the train reached Watford.

Jonathan Rothery lived in a spacious semi-detached house with a large garden a ten-minute walk from the station. He was home when I arrived. I introduced myself to his daughter and she took me to the lounge where her father was watching the news.

He was sitting in his wheelchair with a blanket across his knees. His daughter introduced us.

"You'll forgive me if I don't stand up?" I was impressed he'd still got his sense of humour.

He still had most of his hair, it was chalky grey and short. He was wearing a shirt and tie and had a barrel chest. He was probably a formidable physical presence in his younger days. No longer.

"Why would a Yard Detective Sergeant come all the way out here to see me?" he asked.

"A rather delicate matter, actually." I looked at his daughter. She nodded and left after saying she'd bring some coffees in soon.

"I don't understand," he said when the door closed. He switched the news off.

I explained very briefly what I was investigating and that I was filling in some gaps. I didn't give him much detail, just a few broad strokes.

"You were in the army in the seventies," I began.

"Yeah, I was a squaddie for about thirteen, fourteen years. Came out around the time Thatcher had that parade to celebrate victory in the South Atlantic. I'd loved to have gone on that one. I'd got a licence whilst in the forces so I drove a lorry for a number of years until this," he nodded down at the chair. "Now I sit in one of these bloody things all the time."

There was something about his tone, about his body language that made me think he was ready to spill his guts out. I wondered if he suspected why I was in his home. I continued.

"I want to ask you about something specific that occurred whilst you were still a serving soldier in the mid 1970s."

His expression changed, as though he knew what was coming next. He pursed his lips.

"Okay." He folded his arms.

"I'm investigating a recent case that's led to three deaths and I believe there's a connection to this and something that occurred much earlier. I'll come straight to the point, Mr Rothery." I paused. "In the mid seventies you were part of some quasi-military outfit being trained to mount an action to overthrow the Government. That's correct, isn't it?"

I said this almost accusingly.

He looked at me quite obliquely, almost as if he'd lost his connection with the real world and was struggling to make sense of what was happening outside of him. He glanced out the window but didn't appear to be noticing anything.

"How much do you know?" he finally said.

"I know the broad outline though not the main details. I've seen the manifesto and the pictures of training exercises. I even know the logo *Auspicium Melioris Aevi.*

Good enunciation, eh?" I grinned at him. He didn't appear to be impressed.

"I see," he said resignedly.

"Oh, don't worry. I'm not here to arrest you for it. It didn't happen so there's probably nothing to charge you with anyway. I'm not even sure there's such a charge as retrospective treason. No, my interest in this case is a little more specific. Do you know of someone named Eric Biggins? You know who I'm talking about?"

He was silent for a while, staring at a blank television screen. I suspected he was reliving events he'd thought he'd successfully buried in his subconscious. As if being in a wheelchair wasn't bad enough, now he was experiencing existential angst. His whole demeanour became one of a kind of subdued melancholia, as though he was suffused with sadness. He exhaled.

"I knew Eric."

"So I'm guessing you know what I'm going to ask next," I said. He nodded.

"I think so." He took a deep breath. I waited a moment.

"You were one of the firing squad."

"How do you know that?" He looked surprised.

"Someone who was there."

"Can I know who?"

I shook my head. "'Fraid not."

He sat silent and very still for several seconds. His daughter entered carrying a tray with two coffees. She saw her father's expression. She gave me a look that seemed to say "Go easy on him." I wondered how much she knew and whether she'd realised why I was with her father. She patted him on the arm and left the room. I ignored the coffee.

"There's not a day goes past I don't think of that poor bastard and what was done to him. I actually think I'm in this wheelchair because the Lord is punishing me on earth for what we did."

I took this as his cue to open up.

"Why don't you tell me what happened? Start at the beginning. Take your time."

He sipped his coffee. It seemed to fortify him.

"I always wanted to be a soldier. Proud to be one. Proud to serve in one of the finest fighting units in the whole bloody army," he stated in an even voice. "I really loved being in uniform. Didn't think there was anything better in this world. You ever been a soldier? You ever been in uniform?"

I stated I hadn't, only wore a policeman's uniform for a few years until I became a detective in CID. What had I done, he asked. School, university, the beat, CID and now Special Branch. Served differently but for the same ends. Protection of Queen and Country.

"I joined up in sixty nine, when the world seemed to be full of student agitators campaigning against the Vietnam war. We even had riots in this country. Bloody foreign students whipping up resentments against a war we weren't even part of." He sounded angry.

"Anyway, I did. I tell you, you've not known camaraderie until you've fought alongside someone, seen them in action, seen them react to being under fire and the level of awareness they show. I have. Two tours of duty in Northern Ireland. Both sides hating us."

He shook his head as though he didn't believe what he was saying. Maybe he didn't want to.

I noticed, as he was speaking, his eyes had glazed over. He was talking to and for himself rather than to me. It was almost cathartic for him. Things he'd probably not said to anyone outside of his regiment were now pouring out of him. Had he been bottling up these feelings since leaving the army? I allowed him to continue.

"You ever seen someone shot and die in front of you?" he asked solemnly.

I resisted the flippancy of replying, "Yes, actually, the other night. I was with two young men as they were both shot by an assassin and died.'

--------◄◊►--------

178

"No, I haven't," I lied. "Only the after effects, the clearing up. That sort of thing."

"I have," he stated with all the certainty he could muster. "A couple of my mates in the regiment were shot dead by snipers. On patrol in Belfast we were. Just walking along some shitty backstreet trying to keep the fucking Irish from killing each other. Never caught the bastards who did it either, or if we did we didn't know it. Ireland was a nightmare. We had to use softly-softly against terrorists who were planting bombs beneath cars and killing innocent people. Soldiers were considered expendable. Did you know that?"

I shook my head. No, I didn't know that. How much of this was idle rambling? I allowed him to continue with his musings.

"And when we got back to England, what did we find? Civil war and bloody anarchy 'cause of the unions and a government too weak to stand up to the Commie bastards. Something clearly had to be done, we couldn't go like that."

"Something *was* done, wasn't it?"

He nodded. "Yeah, it was."

He then spent the next few minutes telling me about how he was approached by a senior officer and asked if he wanted to be part of a special Civil Defence unit being secretly trained to help keep the country functioning in the event of any further outbreaks of civil disorder. He agreed to be part of the unit and was taken away from normal duties and trained in a camp somewhere, he thought, in the West Country, to be ready to move in and guard telephone communications premises and power stations so the country could function as normal. That was the story most other soldiers at the camp had been told.

"How long before you discovered what the actual purpose was?"

"I'm not sure. There were all kinds of rumours about revolutions and coups and all that but I didn't take too much notice, to be honest."

"So what did Eric Biggins do to deserve being shot? Did he vote Labour or something?" I was being flippant, hoping to draw Rothery out but he seemed not to hear me. He was silent for about twenty seconds. His eyes moved around and he exhaled a few times. He seemed bothered.

"Funny as it sounds, I don't actually know."

"What, he was just selected at random. Is that it?"

He looked angry for a second. "No, it wasn't that. I heard from some of the lads that Biggins was attempting to blow the whistle on what was happening. Someone said he'd written to a newspaper telling them what was being prepared for. I don't know if that's true, but the next thing I knew, we were gathered together on the parade ground. A major told us we had to be careful as there was a traitor in our midst. Biggins was dragged out to a wall, blindfolded, had his hands tied behind him and, on a count of three, we shot him."

"Christ," I muttered under my breath.

"Funny thing is, we were told our rifles had blanks. I discovered later the bullets were real and Biggins died from gunshot wounds."

"Interesting. The official army record says he died whilst engaged on a training exercise. It's listed as an unfortunate accident. No one was ever blamed for it."

"It wasn't an accident." Rothery was slow and firm in his denial. "We murdered him."

I thought I saw a couple of tears running down his cheek. He was trying to keep himself in check but not succeeding.

"How long afterwards did you find this out?" I ignored the tears.

"Not very long at all. We were expecting him to come back later on that evening but he didn't. Someone asked what had happened. There were all kinds of things being said. Eventually, the major came into the mess and congratulated us on executing a traitor. That's when we realised, or certainly I realised, we'd actually killed someone. I think it was about that point when I began to think this wasn't kosher. There was something about it that wasn't right and I didn't like it."

"What, the private army wasn't just for playing games?" I was hoping to get him agitated.

"With God as my judge I swear I thought what we were doing was preparing to be some kind of beachhead unit to be used in the event of a general strike or civil disturbance. I'd heard the rumours about shooting ministers and all that but I didn't believe them. I mean, come on, this is England. We're not a fucking banana republic, we don't overthrow governments. We're a democracy. We cast votes, that's the British way."

"Did others feel the same as you?"

"Quite a few did. We weren't there to kill anyone. I thought we were being trained for special duties, not to be bloody stormtroopers for a revolution. I tell you, morale certainly went down after that. But we couldn't just walk away, could we?"

"The major you mentioned. His name wasn't Perkins by any chance, was it?"

"Yes, it was. He was the one who welcomed us to the camp, told us about our historic mission and all that crap."

George Selwood had said that I'd be amazed at the extent of the complicity at the top of the establishment at this adventure. He'd mentioned the army and other forces chiefs. I'd never been a soldier but even I knew the army was a total institution. Orders given and orders obeyed without any questioning by the recipients. An officer said shit, you asked if you had to drop your trousers or do it fully clothed. It was beginning to sound as though he was right.

"So, what eventually happened to Eric Biggins' body? Who took care of it?"

"Never knew," he replied slowly, shaking his head. "He was shot and we were ordered away not too long afterwards. That's all I know."

"Ordered away?"

"Yeah, back to our regiments. Whatever we were being prepared for never occurred or, if it did, it went ahead without me." A rare smile.

Quite a story. Perkins had been at the epicentre of the accounts given by George Selwood and now Jonathan Rothery. Both men present at the same time and believing they were being trained to rescue the country they loved from union militancy. Both being exploited by people like Christian Perkins who, it appeared, had another agenda.

"Did you ever know anyone else in command other than Perkins?"

"No. I saw Perkins with a senior officer once but I didn't know who it was. He was only visiting and never spoke to plebs like us."

"And you've no idea why this little escapade never went ahead?"

"None," he replied emphatically. "We were all told we were being RTUed, returned to units, and that was it. It never went ahead, whatever *it* was."

"And you genuinely believed you were being prepared as some kind of Civil Defence force in the event of a general strike or something like that."

He nodded. "Yeah, I did. Most of us there did. That bastard Perkins. We were ordered to keep quiet about this and I have. I've not said anything about this all these years." He waved his hands. "I mean, who'd believe me if I did?" He shrugged. He picked up his coffee and took a lengthy gulp of it.

"So, there it is. It's a big weight off my mind finally telling someone what we did to that poor sod." He paused for a moment. "What happens to me now?"

"Nothing I know of. It's your conscience; you've got to live with yourself. I was just here to pick your brains. I've been told by Perkins that Biggins' death was an accident but you've said it wasn't, so has someone else. But, whatever, that's not what I'm investigating so that's for others to decide. Me? I'm just investigating a case, as I said earlier."

I glanced at my watch. We'd been talking for nearly an hour. It hadn't seemed that long.

"How did all this come to light? We were told all records of the camp and the training were going to be expunged. No one would ever know about it."

Without going into too much detail I explained about discovering the pictures and the manifesto in the course of investigating a blackmail scam. I spoke in generalities and mentioned no names.

"So, Perkins gives the order to shoot. What happens to him?" Rothery asked.

"He got elected to Parliament. What could be worse than that?" I smiled at him. He laughed out loud. I thanked him for his time and insisted that our conversation remains between us. He agreed he would maintain a silence.

Back on the Tube. It was much less crowded and getting a seat was easy. I was idly speculating. Had England really come close to armed insurrection by a brigade of well intentioned, in their own minds, patriots, encouraged and supported by a compliant establishment? Did people like Selwood and Rothery really believe what they'd been told by Perkins? Was this ever a serious likelihood or some foolhardy venture by a small clique of people in the shadows who would gladly wear the fasces to subvert democracy? Would we ever know the whole story?

What I did know was that what had begun a few days back, looking of the movements into Louis Phipps and trying to ascertain why a top-notch assassin had killed him, had now uncovered a whole nest of subterfuge and intrigue.

I still believed Phipps couldn't organise blowing his nose if he had a cold, much less a blackmail scam on someone in Government. Something wasn't adding up.

Friday evening. What was to have been the last night of my

week's holiday, which had instead turned into a work week. I was back in the flat I shared with my partner, Karen. She was out and I was eating a cold pasty and guzzling a cold beer.

I was watching television when the phone rang. It was Mickey.

"You might want to watch the London news later this evening," he began.

"Is it worth it? Who's died?" I enquired.

"Just have a look, eh?"

After a brief chat he rang off.

The local news for London followed the national news. The lead item concerned a public meeting in South West London which had ended in uproar. The speaker was the local MP, Christian Perkins, who'd taken umbrage at a question from a man in the audience who'd asked why he'd been interviewed by a Special Branch detective earlier that day, and did it concern the unlawful death of a soldier under his command in the mid 1970s? He'd refused to answer the question, said that both the question and the questioner were out of order and attempted to continue with his talk, but the questioner had been persistent and asked again, requesting an answer. This aroused the attention of the attendant media. After a while, Perkins had left the platform. A few reporters had asked him what the questioner was talking about and asking him what murder the questioner was referring to, but Perkins had slunk off in a huff, refusing to make any statement. The questioner had also left the building before reporters had caught up with him. Despite repeated requests for clarification, Perkins had not made any statement about the matter to the media. What was to have been a routine public meeting had turned out to be something quite unexpected. It had been quite an evening in South West London.

SIX

Saturday

SMITHERMAN WAS DRESSED casually for a Saturday, which simply meant he'd taken his tie off and hung up his suit jacket. He was reading my reports about who I'd spoken to the day before and progress on the case. I'd included a lot of detail about my talk with Jonathan Rothery.

"So, what I believe is that Louis and Paulie Phipps were both killed because someone didn't want any details of this leaking out into the public domain. I also think Gant was hired by someone who's closely involved in all this. It's either someone in, or close to, the intelligence community. Someone who wanted maximum deniability and didn't want the spooks involved, so he's gone outside and brought in Gant, who is theoretically expendable. He's no connection to us so, worse comes to worse, he gets caught, he can be denied," I summed up.

"And you think Phipps got the pictures and other stuff you've referred to from Debbie Frost's car."

"Yeah, I do. He was pressured to steal the car and give the contents to whoever it was, but this character doesn't want all this stuff, so Phipps sees the chance for a killing. He contacts Debbie Frost and tries to sell it back to her. He winds up dead. Simeon Adaka has the package of stuff until he gives it to me. He too winds up dead. Coincidence?"

"But you don't know who pressed him to steal the car."

"I have my suspicions but nothing that'll stand up in a court of law."

Smitherman put down my report and sat back in his chair.

"CID still haven't come up with an arrest regarding the death of the Phipps. They've talked to a lot of people known

185

to be shooters and who have form but no one can be pointed as a credible suspect. They've either got good alibis or can account for where they were last Monday night."

"There won't be any arrests either," I said in reply. "We both know who pulled the trigger here but can't pin it to him."

"Gant has an alibi for the time in question. MI5 have talked to him and are satisfied with what he told them," Smitherman stated simply.

"Let me guess. His alibi witness is Richard Rhodes."

"Actually, it is." Smitherman sounded surprised. "How did you know that?"

"I spoke to Rhodes last Tuesday morning when I was looking into Gant's motives for going after the Phipps. Says they're friends and always meet up whenever Gant passes through London. I saw them together on CCTV Thursday night at the hotel. Rhodes fits the description of whoever rearranged Simeon Adaka's face for him. I also saw Rhodes with Debbie Frost on Wednesday evening. She, Rhodes and her boyfriend all got out of a cab at her place."

"You're sure it was Rhodes?"

"No mistaking that big bastard. It was definitely him. Yet when I asked Debbie Frost yesterday whether she knew a Richard Rhodes, she didn't seem to think she did."

Smitherman cupped his hands together and touched his chin with his index fingers. His eyes ascended upwards towards the ceiling. He nodded sagely.

"I'm going to show her Rhodes' picture. If she still denies knowing him, I'm going to bring her in."

Smitherman said that was a good idea. He also told me Richard Rhodes had still not been apprehended despite police looking for him after his assaulting Sergeant Bales. That was baffling. He couldn't have left the country without someone alerting the intelligence community. Where could he be hiding?

I drove past the Saturday shoppers through Sloane Square and along the King's Road. The area was crowded with people taking advantage of the unseasonably warm weather. I pulled up at the top of Old Church Street and turned left. I parked in a nearby space and walked along to Mulberry Walk. At the corner I looked along and noticed the front door open. There was a Prius parked on the road with the front door open on the passenger side. I waited.

Five minutes later a man came out to the car, picked up a bag of groceries and went into the house.

I rang the bell marked *Frost-Ritchie* and the same man opened the door. I asked for Debbie. He invited me in and led me up the stairs to their flat. Surprisingly he didn't ask to see any ID.

She was in the small kitchenette making a late breakfast. Something smelled good but I didn't think she'd invite me to join them at their repast.

"Who was it?" she called out.

"You'll never guess," I replied. She turned to face me.

"You again," she snapped. "What now?" She looked about as happy to see me as she would if she'd just been told she had a life-threatening illness.

"Who's this guy?" Darren Ritchie stood next to me. He'd adopted a stroppy tone of voice and I suspected his close proximity was designed to make me feel uncomfortable. I turned and moved towards him. He had to back up to avoid being bumped into.

"I'm a police officer, sunshine." I thrust my ID about an inch from his eyes. He took another step backwards. "You got a problem with that?"

I took an instant dislike to this guy. He was about five ten and thin but very wiry, looking like he might be good at a racquet sport like squash. I hated squash, saw it as a yuppie poseur's game. Hard to believe he'd once been a squaddie.

"What do you want now?" Debbie had put down the tray she was carrying. She was casually dressed in a blue sports sweater and cream coloured sweat pants, and her hair was tied back in a bunch. She looked good, glowing and smelling like she'd just had a shower.

I took a picture from the envelope and showed it to her. "You know this man?" I asked evenly.

"Yeah, I do. Why? What's he done?"

"I asked yesterday if you knew him and you said no."

"You didn't ask me about Richard."

"I definitely did. I asked if you knew Richard Rhodes and you said no," I stated emphatically. I was fed up being misled by her. Maybe I should threaten to arrest her.

"I still don't. The man in that picture is Richard Perkins. Who's Richard Rhodes?"

"What?" I exclaimed. I was staggered. "Richard Perkins?"

I did a quick mental recall in my head and remembered the file I'd seen when first looking into Richard Rhodes' background. There'd been no mention of a father in his army details. It couldn't be, could it? I began to feel uncomfortable.

"Is he any relation to?"

"He is," she interrupted me. "He's Christian Perkins' son."

"Jesus." I shook my head. The son of Christian Perkins. "You're absolutely sure about this?"

"What do you think?" She gave me a look of withering scorn. "'Course I'm sure. I work with the man. I've known him since Oxford. I would certainly know if he had a son, don't you think?"

This wasn't what I was expecting. I'd hoped she wouldn't recognise the picture so I could collar her for lying and obstructing justice; but, not only had she done so, she'd thrown me off track somewhat with this revelation. I regained my composure.

"Do you know where this Richard guy is now? He's wanted for questioning concerning an assault on a police officer last Thursday night."

"I don't, no, I'm afraid not," she said. "I've not seen him

for some while. He's not always in the country, you know. He works abroad."

"No, honey." I was deliberately patronising her now." I think what you meant to say was you've not seen him since last Wednesday night when he left here."

She looked annoyed. Darren Ritchie even more so. He snorted and shuffled on his feet as though he was thinking of moving. He didn't.

"Left here?" she said incredulously. She was irritated. Good.

"Yeah, left here. You all arrived in a taxi around 10.30pm and Rhodes, or whatever his name is, left soon after. I watched you all get out the cab. I asked the driver and he said he'd picked you three up by Green Park. I even have the taxi driver's licence number."

Actually I didn't but they weren't to know that.

"I saw it. I was over the road." I nodded at the window. "Saw Rhodes come in and I saw him leave. You wouldn't know the truth if it stood close enough to kiss you." I sneered as I said this to her. "I think you're a lying bitch."

I was out of order with that comment but, suitably riled, she might just let something important slip out. I was hoping she would.

"Hey, copper or not," Ritchie said loudly. He moved towards me threateningly.

"One more step," I pointed at him, "and you're nicked. You too, sweetheart." I looked at Debbie Frost. She looked forlorn. Her Saturday was not going to plan.

"I know the kind of work this character does when he's abroad." I held up the picture. "He's a merc, a paid killer. You're aware, aren't you, he was implicated in an attack on a hotel in Lebanon last year where a number of women and children died?"

Both Debbie and lover boy stood still and said nothing.

"Does your employer know about Christian Perkins' little boy, about what he does for a living? How would that go down with the party faithful? Is that what's being hidden here?"

Debbie didn't respond.

"Ask Christian if you think I'm lying. He's connected with British Intelligence," I slid the picture back in the envelope, "but you know that already, don't you? Do you know this guy's friend, Phil Gant?"

I was looking directly at her as I spoke. For a second her eyelids moved, as though she was surprised at hearing something unexpected.

"Yeah, as I thought." I left them to their cold breakfast.

Back in the car. Richard Rhodes, the son of Christian Perkins. That had really taken me by surprise.

I radioed the office and asked for the address of the mother of the guy I knew as Richard Rhodes. I was given a Shoreditch address. Using the siren, I managed to reach her flat in only thirteen minutes. I caught her at home. I showed her my ID, asked to speak to her briefly about her son and she invited me into the flat.

I guessed she was close to 60 but was too polite to ask her real age. She was surprised that a police officer would want to talk to her about her son. "What's he done now?"

"Well, to be frank, I'm more concerned about his father," I said.

"His father?" she said flatly.

I glanced around her neat and very tidy little flat but could see no pictures of either Christian Perkins or Richard Rhodes.

"Yeah. I'd just like you to confirm something for me. Richard's father *is* Christian Perkins, isn't he?" I asked in a sympathetic tone. I was wishing a female officer was with me.

She sat still for a few moments. She then reached for her bag, took out a packet of cigarettes and lit one up.

"I knew this would come out one day. Told him it would.

You can't keep something like this a secret forever. I told them both that," she said neutrally.

"Oh, don't worry, I'm not going to broadcast it. Nobody'll know who doesn't need to. I just needed to know as both names have arisen in a case I'm investigating. I was told who Richard's father was and I didn't believe it, so I was just seeking confirmation."

"Well, believe it, because it's true."

For the next ten minutes she told me her story. She'd been working for the Conservative Party at its Smith Square head office as an administrative assistant in the late 1970s. During the run up to the 1979 election she began working longer hours as there was much to do at the office to help keep the party machine ticking over. She met an up-and-coming young man named Christian Perkins who was helping to organise the campaigning. They worked closely together for a while and, a few weeks before the election, they'd had an affair. She'd broken it off but, around the same time, she discovered she was pregnant. Determined not to seek a termination she'd approached Perkins to help out as the father. But he was more concerned with his public image and his reputation inside the party so he offered her a one-off cash settlement of five thousand to keep the matter out of the public eye. She agreed to take it and signed a confidentiality clause prohibiting her from ever mentioning the affair to anyone. She'd raised Richard on her own and, in her view, had done a good job raising a headstrong boy who'd later joined the army and, after leaving, was now working as a "Security Consultant" for a firm in London.

"And that's the story," she concluded. "I'd wanted to make a career in politics but that was lost when Richard was born. Being a single mother back then was a lot different than it is now. I was a fool to have taken that money from him. Bastard. He was more concerned about his sodding career than about his son. He's a bloody MP now, if you will, lording it up in Westminster."

"You realise that gagging order was probably never legally binding? You could have got out of it any time had you wanted."

"Maybe, but it's too late to worry about that now." She sounded bitter. I didn't blame her.

"Where did the name Rhodes come from?"

"My maiden name. Mary Rhodes."

"Did Richard have any contact at all with his father growing up?"

"Not through me he didn't."

"I believe Richard and his father are now reconciled. I think they spend time together, if I've heard right."

"Could be," she shrugged.

"How would he have found out who his father was if there was a gagging order?"

"I don't know. I just know that, a few years ago, he came home and said he'd finally found out who his natural father was. He was pleased about it as well, but how they eventually got together I can't tell you because I don't know."

The flat was small. It was hard imagining a big guy like Richard Rhodes growing up in such a small environment.

"Who's he a consultant with? Do you know which firm?"

She paused for a moment to think.

"I think they're called "Prevention," or something like that."

I realised I knew who she meant.

"You mean *Prevental*?"

"Yes, that's the name," she replied eagerly. "He must be doing good work there as they keep sending him abroad to do work for them."

I wasn't going to disillusion Mary Rhodes and tell her that, *au contraire*, her son was a fully trained merciless killer who fought for money in places he had no official business being in, and being somehow implicated in three recent deaths, as well as being wanted for an assault on a police officer. If she was ever going to learn the truth about her son, it would not be from me.

"Yes, it does sound like that, doesn't it?" I agreed with her. I stood.

"He's a good son, Officer. He always comes to see me when he's back in the country." The pride in her voice was noticeable.

I thanked her for her time and left her to her memories. It was almost heart-warming knowing that even a thug like Richard Rhodes was loved by his old mum, who saw him as a good boy. The love of a good woman indeed.

In the car, I noticed I had a missed call from Mickey on my mobile. I called him.

"Ol' Perkins got a bit pissed with my questions. You should have seen him; looked like he wanted to spit blood. There were a number of journalists there and they looked amazed at his response. When I asked him again he just walked off stage with journalists asking him what the question was about, but he wouldn't answer. He went off. One of them tried asking me what I was really asking but I brushed him aside and left."

"Thanks, mate, you did a good job."

"It's even made the press. You seen it?"

With all the excitement going on I hadn't looked at today's papers. Being a Saturday I'd have probably only looked at the football and rugby news, especially now as the season for both was drawing to a close. I admitted I'd not seen a paper today.

"Perkins' meeting last night has got a mention in a couple of the broadsheets. The *Telegraph* said something about controversy at a Tory MP's constituency meeting because of a question asked about his being interviewed by a Special Branch detective earlier in the day. Perkins didn't answer and left the meeting hall." Mickey sounded proud of his evening's work. "What's he actually done then, this guy?"

"Long story, but suffice to say he's got a bit of an unsavoury past and I think he could be involved in those shootings outside your place last Monday."

"What, an MP with an unsavoury past? Never !"

"Yeah, who knew, eh? I'm trying to nail him on some aspect of it but so far there's no direct proof. I've got an idea what might be happening which I'm going to investigate."

"You want me for anything else?"

I said no, thanked him for last night and rang off.

I'd managed to get under Perkins' skin and he had no idea he'd been set up. Good. I was anxious to see what else would transpire.

Coming up for lunchtime and I was at my desk checking something. I saw a note asking me to call *New Focus* magazine. Now, who could that be? I had no doubt what he wanted to talk about and I knew it wouldn't be to offer an invite to Sunday lunch with him and his in-laws. Richard Clements was at his desk when I got through.

"Rob, thanks for returning my call. What's going on with Christian Perkins? Media's really running with this one. *The Guardian* said something about him refusing to answer a question about someone unlawfully killed whilst he was in charge of some squad or other. Paper also said he'd been spoken to by someone in Special Branch about it. You perchance?" he asked almost longingly.

"It's part of an ongoing investigation into what was originally a case involving two murders but now involves three. I can't comment on the case."

"So it *was* you." He sounded certain.

"Told you, I can't comment. You could ask your father-in-law. He might help you."

"Him?" Clements gasped. "He thinks I'm only one rung above a child molester. Thinks I'm a bad influence on democracy. Got no time for a free press or anyone who does what I do. Straight up. A while back, he took me to one side and asked whether you were my source for that story in *The Observer*. Said it was obvious someone had to have helped me put it together and he wanted to know who. I said it wasn't you and that, anyway, I don't give up the names of anyone who's a source on a story."

I was glad it wasn't an invite to Sunday lunch. Sitting between Clements and Smitherman was about as appealing as a kick in the groin.

"So, I can't help you, I'm afraid," I stated.

"Would it be worth my while looking into Christian Perkins' past?"

"You're the journalist. I can't tell you who to look into," I said, hoping he'd read between the lines.

"Well, thanks for calling back," he said. With his range of contacts I was hoping between them they could dig up something to make Perkins squirm.

I'd been in the office because I wanted to log onto the Border Agency site checking to see if Phil Gant had left the country. No one by that name was registered as having left so I assumed he was still at the same Park Lane hotel.

However, I did discover that Richard Perkins had left the country yesterday on a flight from Stansted to Schiphol, Amsterdam, no doubt to resume duties with the Colombians. He'd travelled under his father's name. No one was looking for Richard Perkins. He'd slipped the net.

Back along Grosvenor Place, around Hyde Park Corner and north up Park Lane, this time with no siren, just a leisurely cruise through the streets of London on a sunny Saturday lunchtime. I did a U-turn at a traffic island, drawing a few scowls from taxi drivers as I turned, and pulled up outside Gant's hotel. An officious looking jobsworth in full maroon uniform with gold braiding plus a peaked cap began walking towards me. He had an expression suggesting he'd just swallowed a wasp. Perhaps it was indignation at my temerity in parking where six-figure Rolls-Royces usually stood. I flashed my ID without even looking in his direction and went up the steps into the foyer, leaving him to choke on his wasp.

I showed my ID to the woman at the reception desk and asked if a Mr Gant was still registered as a guest. He was. She said he was currently taking tea in the lounge bar and was booked in to use the hotel sauna room at 2pm. I asked her to do something for me and she said she would. I then walked to the bar. He was there, sat in a corner glancing at a copy of the *Herald Tribune*. I approached him. He looked up and, seeing me, did a double take. He folded the paper and smiled at me. I sat opposite on what was a luxuriously upholstered chair. I could get used to taking afternoon tea sitting on one of these.

"So, this is what you look like in daylight. I've only ever seen you in the dark." He grinned at me. "Actually your picture doesn't do you justice. Must have been an old one."

I didn't ask where he'd seen a picture of me. I knew where it came from.

"Keep a copy for yourself, did you?" I said straight faced.

"What do you need, Officer?" Straight down to business. He was looking as though his remaining seated to answer my questions was a sacrifice on his part. From his accent I was guessing he was from New England.

"How much did Christian Perkins pay you to take out Louis and Paulie Phipps? Must be quite a sum as it's not cheap to stay here," I said casually, looking at the opulent surroundings. "What's it cost, a thousand a night? More?"

"Christian Perkins? Who might he be?" His American accent was more noticeable now.

"The man who hired you. He told me. Told me he'd got in touch with you through his son, whom I'm told you know." I paused for a few moments. "Richard Rhodes? An old comrade-in-arms from your days in the Lebanon? Surely you remember an old war buddy."

He nodded. It was clear from his body language he recognised the names I'd given him.

"I've gotta give you credit for the two shots. Took out two people in a heartbeat *and* in the dark. Impressive. Where did you fire from? CID combed the area but couldn't come up with where they thought the shots might have come from. They're not even certain what kind of weapon was used. You used that hybrid you showed me, didn't you?" I said calmly.

We were both at ease, sitting comfortably and looking relaxed. Looked at from across the bar we were just two old friends having a chat over a pot of tea. No differences between us, except he was impeccably dressed and I wasn't, and the price of his tea would be the cost of a two person Chinese takeaway for me. The only way I could stay here overnight would be to hide in a storage space and hope I wasn't discovered.

He was cool. What I'd said hadn't fazed him in the slightest. I had no evidence Perkins was involved in any way, but it stood to reason he had to be there somewhere along the line, and I couldn't see any other way the case was going to break, so I was idly speculating.

"Here …" I took out my mobile phone. "Call him. Ask him why he told me about your involvement in the two deaths. You told me yourself a client's business is always confidential but, about an hour or so ago, Christian Perkins told me he'd hired you to eliminate two people who were trying to extort money from a woman he knows. You want me to call him for you? I have his number."

His expression changed slightly. He knew and I knew. There was some slight change in his demeanour. He looked down at his tea but quickly regained his composure. He was a pro. Someone like me wasn't going to entrap him as easy as that. But I'd struck a chord. My theory about how the case had gone down wasn't as wide of the mark as I'd feared it might be. Sometimes it's better to be lucky than good.

My synopsis was that the package with the photos and manifesto belonged to Perkins. I still wasn't sure how they'd ended up in Debbie Frost's car, but Louis Phipps had stolen the car containing them under pressure from someone. Was Perkins that someone? He'd then tried to sell them back to her and, not too long afterwards, had wound up dead. Perkins, through Richard Rhodes, had hired Gant to kill the Phippses. There were still a few dots I couldn't join up but a picture of sorts was slowly beginning to take shape.

"If what you say is true, you'd be here arresting me." He smiled and tilted his head slightly at me. It read like a smile that said, in another reality, I'd kill you stone dead someplace quiet. "You wouldn't just be here giving me some goddamn bullshit story about a couple of people I know. You'd be slapping the cuffs on me and taking me off somewhere. That's the real position, isn't it?"

"I'm just wondering how a Member of Parliament would come to know a stone killer like you?"

"Richard's his son. I know Perkins through him. In actual fact I'm meeting him here quite soon so I'm afraid our little chat will have to be curtailed. Sorry." He picked up his delicate bone china cup and finished drinking. He stood. I did too.

"Ah, ah." I shook my head. "You're a material witness to an assault on a Police officer last Thursday evening. I'd like you to come with me to West End Central and give a statement."

I didn't tell him Rhodes had left the country.

"Huh?"

"Two nights back, a police officer was assaulted in the lobby of a hotel whilst in the execution of his lawful duties. It was caught on CCTV. You're clearly identified in that picture. You're in a position to help with our enquiries." I never tired of using that phrase.

He stood motionless for a few moments considering his options. He sniggered, said "Jesus," and tried to move past me. I blocked his exit.

"You're not leaving," I said.

At that moment the two security guards on duty, both big ex-police officers, came over. One stood behind Gant, the other stood next to me, eyes fixed on him. I'd asked the receptionist to have security ready in case it was needed. She'd done her job. The one behind patted Gant down, searching for weapons. He didn't find anything. Gant sat down again looking amused.

I dialled my office and asked for back-up. Five minutes later three Special Branch detectives plus another man I didn't recognise turned up. I nodded towards Gant.

"Take him in. Hold him. Keep him away from everyone. He and I are going to have a nice little chat, aren't we?" I smiled at him. "He's going to tell me the secrets of the universe."

"Actually, DS McGraw, my department has an interest in this man. I think we'll take it from here," the other man said.

"Okay, you know where to take him." He nodded to the other officers. They led Gant away though he wasn't cuffed.

"Who are you?" I was annoyed. I knew the answer whilst asking the question.

"Nicholson, MI5," he stated for the record. "Gant's our man now. We need to talk to him about some matters of interest to us and then it'll be decided what happens to him."

"Gant killed two men last Monday night. Is he walking away from that?"

"Now, you know I can't discuss operations details with persons not in my section, any more than you can. Special Branch will be appraised when it's deemed expedient to do so. Thank you for your cooperation." He turned and followed the others out of the bar. I was aware that all the lunchtime diners in the bar were watching the drama unfold. I went back to my car.

I returned to the Yard, parked the car and walked back to Christian Perkins' flat. It was still warm and there were lots of tourists looking at maps and excitedly pointing to the outer walls of Buckingham Palace at the top of the road.

I was hoping he was in. I was going to relay to him my

synopsis of how I thought things had gone, as well as clueing him in on where his friend Phil Gant now was and what was happening to him.

After the events of the previous evening there were several journalists, photographers and a TV news team outside the entrance to his block of flats, which suggested he was in residence. A couple of the journalists looked at me as I entered but, deciding I looked insignificant, let me pass without question.

Perkins let me in as soon as he saw me outside his door. He seemed almost pleased to see me.

"Those hyenas still out there?" he asked.

I said there were a few gentlemen of the press outside wishing to ask him about last night's meeting and his refusal to answer a question from a member of the public, if that's who he meant. I smiled as I told him that. He didn't appreciate my weak humour.

He seemed as though he had the weight of the world on his broad shoulders. He was radiating an air of melancholia. The arrogance and confidence he'd exhibited yesterday were nowhere to be seen. He slumped down into an armchair.

"Who was the man who asked that question?" He looked straight at me. "I didn't recognise him and he left almost immediately afterwards. Very strange. I've got the bloody press all over me on this. How would he have known that?"

"I wasn't there and I don't know." I kept a straight face. At least, I hoped it was straight.

He sighed and shook his head. He reminded me of a school kid who'd been caught by the headteacher and was finally resigned to accepting his fate. I went straight for the jugular.

"Are you aware Phil Gant was arrested by Special Branch forty minutes ago? MI5 have now got him, I'm guessing they're holding him at Century whilst they decide what's to be done with him. My guess? He'll be ferried out the country. They'll get rid of him until they want his services again. The two guys he killed? That'll get ignored. In the greater scheme of things, their lives will be considered an irrelevance. What do you think?"

He said nothing in reply. He was in deep repose, considering his own future. His eyes betrayed confusion and he looked tired.

"I think those two bodies I just mentioned are down to you. You hired Gant to take them out, didn't you? Why didn't you use your son? He'd have killed them for nothing. I'll bet you had to pay Gant a fortune, didn't you?" I paused. "Richard would have enjoyed killing them because he's a sadistic thug. You agree?"

At the mention of the name Richard, he looked up at me for a couple of seconds and then averted his eyes.

There was a lengthy silence. Perkins looked around the room. He looked at everything as if he didn't recognise anything and was wondering where he was and how he got there.

"How does Debbie Frost figure in all this? What's her role?"

He turned to stare at me. Mentioning her name had got his attention.

"The pictures I showed you yesterday came from a package that was in her car when it was stolen earlier this year," I continued. "I think it's your package though I don't know why it was in her car, and she even denies there was anything there, despite three people losing their lives over it. That's a lot of people dying over something she says doesn't exist. What do you think?"

He rubbed his eyes and continued sitting and staring partly at me and partly at the wall behind me. I wondered which he found the more interesting. Was he even listening?

"Her car was stolen because it was targeted. Someone who knew where she was going to be at that time paid Louis and Paulie Phipps to steal it. Someone like you, perhaps? Whoever it was then took something and left everything else behind. Phipps decided to try and cash in and he contacted Debbie Frost about what he had in his possession, though again I'm not sure who told him it was valuable. Phipps is arrested but he gets interviewed by a DCI Tomkinson and he also gets seen by two MI5 spooks. Quite an array of talent to be involved in a routine car theft, wouldn't you say? Or was there something more sinister involved? Who would have told MI5 about it?"

He maintained his silence.

"Louis Phipps said he'd been pressured into stealing the car by a police officer who told him he'd go down unless he did what they wanted. He was also told he'd not go to prison for it. That would take what Americans call juice. You have juice, don't you?" I stated. "I don't accept what Phipps did was random. I believe his claim to have been pressured into acting. Left to himself he wouldn't know how to pick his own nose. Someone was using him. You, maybe?"

He smiled but still said nothing.

"Was this whole thing about covering up your involvement in some attempted coup and having an innocent soldier shot?"

He grinned when I mentioned that.

"Let me know when I'm boring you too much," I said nonchalantly after a twenty-second gap.

"Oh, no, you're not boring me at all. Some very perceptive questions."

He stood up and walked into the kitchen, took two cups from the shelf and poured coffee into both. He gave one to me and sat down again. I sipped mine. Freshly filtered. It was good coffee.

"You just can't prove any of it, can you?" He smirked. "This is all conjecture on your part. You have a few basic facts and you've added some gloss to them. It's riveting stuff but it goes nowhere really, does it?" He sounded more alive, as though I'd touched a chord somewhere inside of him and he was responding to its reverberating.

"If, as you said, those pictures proved nothing, why was someone so concerned to prevent knowledge of them being circulated?" I asked. "I've spoken to someone who thought the shooting of Eric Biggins was just a laugh, a wind-up, but who's since discovered it was the real thing. That's murder as far as I'm concerned. Is that what's being covered up?"

He said nothing. I stood up.

"We'll continue this at the Yard. I think you're lying and I'm sick of being lied to, so I'm taking you in. That'll give the press something to talk about outside when we walk past together with you in handcuffs, won't it?" I said. "Christian Perkins, I'm arresting you on suspicion of being party to a conspiracy to commit murder. You don't have to say—"

"You're not serious, are you?" He sounded worried. "You really going to do this? This goes higher than me. The whole thing does."

"Okay, convince me. You tell me what this is all about and I might reconsider this course of action. Otherwise I guarantee you'll be in custody before you can say *Auspicium Melioris Aevi*. Like my pronunciation?" I smiled at him. He ignored me.

He sat down again. He somehow seemed more in control of himself. It was just a guess but I now had the impression he was more focused. He was still agitated about the situation but now had the chance to play things his way. I sat down at the table nearby.

"Okay, talk to me." I was ready. He took a deep breath and sighed.

"Your initial comments yesterday were correct. There *was* a plan to overthrow the Labour Government but it came from a source you'd not believe and, even now, is classified top secret and buried deep within the Whitehall labyrinth and very likely will never see the light of day. But there was a wider purpose than what you might think."

"And that was?"

"Top secret," he said matter-of-factly and shaking his

head, as though it was obvious and didn't need spelling out. "The real reason for it all was successful, and that's all you get to know."

He looked out the window for a few moments, gathering his thoughts.

"I won't bore you with the details but, suffice to say, what was being planned was ultimately in the best interests of the country."

"So your manifesto was right when it said union bosses and Government ministers were to be rounded up and shot," I asked outright. "It was a definite plan."

"Oh, absolutely. No doubt at all. But it was all just a front for the real reason."

"Which was?"

"As I just said, Detective, you will never know. It's a very closely guarded secret and will stay that way, quite likely for evermore. I doubt even the hundred years rule will apply."

This wasn't going as I'd planned. He was admitting to what George Selwood had told me but was now saying it was not for the reasons given.

"What about Eric Biggins? What sins did he commit?"

"Ah, Eric. He was going to leak what was happening. He was part of why the whole plan was set up, *ab initio*. That we couldn't allow, so he was dealt with military style, by firing squad. I took full responsibility for the safety of what was being planned and I was exonerated."

"By whom?"

He smiled and shook his head.

"So this was a lawful killing." I said, hoping to be corrected. I wasn't.

"It was. I don't regret what was done as it was ultimately successful. Trust me, if we hadn't done it, someone else would have done."

Perkins looked proud when he said this. He was enjoying recounting adventures that occurred almost forty years ago. I thought for a few moments.

"So this coup, or whatever, never occurred because—" I speculated.

"Because it was never intended to. There was never going to be one. The whole thing was a counter-deception – the manifesto, training a private army and all that. It was designed to make certain people in various Government offices think it was going to happen. Once they believed that, those individuals the security services had an interest in came out of the woodwork and they were hauled in." He smirked with self-satisfaction.

"And it's not worth my while asking, is it?" I asked hopefully.

"I'm afraid not. Sorry."

I thought for a moment.

"So you're saying this coup, or whatever, was never going to occur. It was a scheme by security to smoke person or persons unknown out of wherever they were hiding?"

"Without being too specific, that's the situation. And it worked."

"Is this why the Phippses were killed? Because they'd found all this out?"

"Couldn't take the chance on what they knew. You were right earlier. It was myself and Richard who, ah, persuaded them to act for us. They stole the car all right, but they opened the bags and found the pictures, plus some other sensitive items, one of which was personal. I took the really important materials. You don't need to know what. The rest was of no consequence and could easily be dismissed if they ever surfaced. Phipps, however, thought otherwise, and tried selling them to Debbie Frost. At that point I didn't know what he did or didn't know. Richard said he'd take care of it. Enter Mr Gant. The rest, as they say, is history."

"So that's why MI5 came in on their interview." I looked directly at Perkins.

"Right," he nodded. "Needed to know what they knew."

"How did Phipps know who was who or what it was all about?"

"She told him. She met him and paid for the return of the pictures and the rest of it, but he reneged on it. Wanted more. Threatened to go to the newspapers. He'd photo-copied everything and was going to tell the press what he'd seen. One of the items he kept was a letter she wrote to me which Phipps saw, and it contained something I didn't want revealed. He was going to name me and her. Couldn't have that." He shook his head vigorously.

"So Debbie Frost did lose a package from her car when it was stolen."

"She did indeed and I wanted it back so that's why I, ah, persuaded the Phippses to go and steal her car for me."

"Because you knew she had them there."

"I did." He nodded his agreement.

"How did she get hold of them?" I was curious.

"Long story. The potted version?" He spread his hands. "She and I had an affair a while ago. I've known her a long time. I knew her when she was a student up at Oxford, you know?"

"I know. I've seen pictures."

He appeared momentarily surprised but continued.

"I've carried a torch for her for years. I arranged to get her the job at Central Office. It usually goes to someone older with more experience but I pulled a few strings and she got it. I kept in touch and we began an affair a couple of years ago. It was the greatest love I've ever known but I couldn't leave my wife, you see? Would have destroyed my career, a man my age and her?"

His eyes looked almost pleading with me to understand; two men of the world together.

"And we couldn't have that, now, could we?" My sarcasm was noticeable. I cared nothing for his feelings.

I remembered Richard Clements telling me Debbie Frost had had an affair with a leading Tory but I would never have guessed it was with Christian Perkins. He was more than twice her age and had children the same age as her. A father fixation perhaps? Was he simply a useful conduit for her to get to the top of the greasy pole? Could it even have been love? Who knew?

"Anyway, I broke it off last autumn. Just before last Christmas, though, she tells me she's pregnant and the child's mine. Neither of us was happy at the idea of a child so she decided she'd have an abortion. Phipps saw a letter she wrote telling me she was pregnant and wanted to know what we were going to do about the situation. I knew where and when it was going to happen so, when I knew she was going to be undergoing the procedure, I arranged for her car to be stolen."

"She had the pictures by then? Where'd she get them from?"

"Took the break-up badly. Became hysterical. Threatened to go to the press." He was talking almost mechanically, as though reciting a script he'd rehearsed beforehand. "We managed to get things sorted out, but not before she stole the package with the pictures and all the other evidence."

"Where from?"

"My house. My constituency's Richmond and I've a house by Wimbledon Common. She was there quite often so she knew her way around."

"How did she know about them?"

"I told her. Stupid thing to do, I know, but I ended up telling her about the plan. Not the whole thing, you understand, not the real reason. She was impressed. When we broke up she went there and stole the package whilst I was away. She was going to use them as leverage to get back together with me."

"How did you get on to Louis Phipps? How did you know him?"

"Didn't. Got a friend in the police to do some research and find a stooge. His name came up. I took him to one side, told him I could have him thrown inside unless he did what I wanted. Scared him half to death, it did." He seemed pleased by that. "Told him what I wanted and he did it. I took a few things out of the package, the really incriminating material. I was a fool. Should have taken the whole thing but I left them behind. Phipps finds them and tries to sell them to Debbie, thinking they're hers."

"So that's when you got on to Gant," I said.

"Me? Good Lord, no." He stressed this point. "It wasn't me who did that. That was her. She arranged for Gant to kill the Phippses. She was correcting her mistake in telling Phipps what this was all about, and for his being a lying little shit. I had nothing to do with that."

"Debbie Frost hired Gant?" I was surprised yet, at the same time, I wasn't.

He nodded. "Yes, Detective, she most certainly did."

"How would she know about him and where to contact him?"

"Through my son, Richard. She knew him through me and she got in touch with him asking if he knew anyone prepared to do a killing for her, and he introduced her to Gant. I'm not sure why but Gant owed them a favour and he said he'd take care of the problem."

"A favour." I repeated.

"Yes. Gant did it for free."

"It was Rhodes who went turning over Phipps' flat looking for that package, wasn't it?"

"Quite likely. I would imagine so. Sounds like his style."

"It was also him who killed Simeon Adaka last Thursday, wasn't it." I wasn't asking.

Perkins said nothing. He sat still and looked nonplussed.

No wonder Gant had smiled when I'd accused Perkins of hiring him when it had been Miss Sweet and Innocent herself, Debbie Frost. Could I arrest her on what I had?

"So, this whole thing was because she got mad at you, stole a package from you, you get Phipps to steal it back to get what you want. He keeps the rest, tries to sell it back to her and gets himself killed in the process. Three dead because you and her fell out."

"Neatly summarised, Detective. That's largely how this sorry situation arose. She really made a pickle of it all, I'm afraid. If she'd only kept her mouth shut." His voice got lower and he stopped talking.

"Biggins and the Phipps brothers, plus Simeon Adaka. Four dead and your grubby handprints on all four bodies. You denying any responsibility for them?"

"Oh, I'm probably culpable in some way, I would imagine," he said serenely.

Perkins drained his coffee.

"Phipps was actually shrewder than you'd give him credit for. He saw a chance to make money and went for it. Alas, however . . ." His voice died away.

"Are you prepared to put all this into a sworn statement?" I asked.

"Good heavens no." His voice sounded as if I'd asked the most stupid question ever. "And I shall deny ever saying a word of this if it ever comes out in public. As I said, I've been a fool but I've not killed anyone."

"You want to tell that to Eric Biggins' family? You even went to his funeral, didn't you? You had him killed then stood there with his family whilst they mourned their son and buried him."

"Buried with full honours and his memory unbesmirched. If they knew the truth—" He stopped.

"Anyway, that's why Stimpson saw your DCI Smitherman recently, to put him in the picture. You may soon find your investigation will go no further, Detective." He looked smug.

"I've got to hand it to you, Perkins, you're a real piece of work. No wonder your son's an amoral piece of shit. I wonder which parent he gets that from?"

"Don't judge me, Detective. You're not capable of doing it properly." He used a patronising tone , as though I was just a hired hand asking to perform a task I was unqualified for. "If you knew the whole story you wouldn't be so quick to condemn me."

As Perkins was speaking, the door to his flat opened and three men entered. I recognised the one in front. It was Stimpson, whom I'd seen recently in Smitherman's office. He walked to where I was now standing. The other two men stood by Perkins.

"You just don't understand, do you?" Perkins said airily, smiling and shaking his head.

"We meet again, DS McGraw," Stimpson began. "It was entirely predictable you'd come here to talk to our colleague, Mr Perkins."

"Colleague?" I looked at Perkins.

"Yes, Detective, colleague. You know, someone you work alongside?" He sounded condescending. I was irritated. I wanted to hit him.

"Mr Perkins has to come with us as we need to talk to him," he continued. "I think we can safely say your involvement in this case is now concluded, DS McGraw. I believe you'll find there'll be no further investigation into this matter." He said this in an amiable voice, almost as if he was politely turning down an offer I'd made for us to play golf. "DCI Smitherman will put you in the picture."

As he spoke the two other men and Perkins walked out of the flat. Perkins looked back at me for a second then followed the other two out.

"Down to the basement and out the back, in case you were wondering about our exit strategy," Stimpson said calmly. "There's a car waiting for us. The press outside will not know Perkins isn't in residence as they won't have seen him leave."

I didn't reply. I left the flat, followed closely by Stimpson. He closed the door behind him. We didn't talk descending the stairs. He continued past the ground floor down to the basement. I walked out past the newshounds who, once again, ignored me. I was used to being ignored.

I walked back to the office and wrote up an account of all that had happened that day and deposited a copy on Smitherman's desk. He wasn't there so I left it and began to pack up. I was feeling flat and dejected. I'd been confident we were near to resolving the case and getting the cuffs on somebody but that now appeared highly unlikely.

I was sure I now knew how things had gone concerning the deaths of Louis and Paulie Phipps but I could prove nothing. Courts of Law don't convict on conjecture and opinion. Both of these I had plenty of but nothing in the way of solid evidence that counsel could pin on someone and get a conviction based upon it.

I was especially dejected about Debbie Frost's role. She'd stonewalled me all week, had blatantly lied to me and been obstructive, yet she was now probably going to walk free and continue her climb up the Conservative Party ladder, from a position her boyfriend had wangled for her. The Phipps brothers, especially Louis, may well have been about as much use to society as a virulent strain of bacteria, but even they deserved to know their assailants had paid the price for unlawfully taking their lives to cover up something potentially politically embarrassing if it were made public. Barring something unforeseen, that wasn't going to happen.

Even worse, this past week was supposed to have been a week's holiday but, instead, I'd spent it looking into a pair of murders I was a witness to but had been unable to resolve because, somehow, the case had crossed over into 'National Security as defined by MI5' territory. I didn't know when I'd reached that point. Maybe I never would. Smitherman may or may not tell me, assuming he ever knew the situation. I was frustrated and needed an outlet for my anger. I knew where to find it.

Prevental had its offices in Mayfair on the top two floors above an upmarket clothing store, not too far from the American Embassy. It was a high-powered security consultancy business providing everything from nightwatchmen to mercenary soldiers, though from its blurb, you'd never guess. Its website was so anodyne it could appear in a daytime soap opera.

I was admitted into the building and went to the second floor. I asked to speak to Gavin Dennison. Told he was in a meeting I said I'd wait downstairs for him. I was asked my name and I said Phil Gant. I was interested to see if he came out when he heard that name.

I'd waited across the street for about fifteen minutes when I saw him come outside. He looked around for who he thought he was going to meet. As he looked around he saw me walking across the street towards him. He smiled.

"Rob, how you doing?" He sounded pleasantly surprised. "I'm just meeting someone."

"That'd be me, pal."

I walked straight into him, grabbed his tie by the knot, pushed my clenched fist up again his throat and shoved him into the nearby wall. Hard. He made a noise that sounded like "Ercke". I kept my fist on his throat and pushed hard. He was clearly in discomfort and I had the edge.

I stared at him for a few moments. He struggled to break my grip but couldn't. I wanted to punch him in the mouth then wipe my feet on him when he was down, but I resisted the desire. I gave him a final push in the throat and released my grip. I stepped back. He rubbed his throat and tried to regain his composure.

"What the fuck's your problem?" He was angry.

"Monday night, when Gant phoned here, he gave someone a description and was told it was me. Only one person here would know that: you. You told him, didn't you?" I hissed.

"He's a client. He's registered with us. He's entitled to ask what he did. Yeah, he said where the bar was and described who was going in. I know you and Corsley are friends and it made sense from the description that it was you. What about it?"

"Gant killed two people just after that and he's going to get away with it," I said. "You helped him."

"Gant, people like him, they're untouchable, Rob. You know the kind of work they do and who they do it for. Christ, mate, are you really that naïve?" He said this almost sorrowfully, shaking his head. "Is that what all this is about?"

"No," I shook my head. "No, it's not that."

"What is it then?"

"It's people like you that piss me off. Helping people like Gant and your friend Paul Farrier to flout the laws in this country and assume they can do so because they don't apply to them. Two people died needlessly because some bitch got mad at her boyfriend and stole something which could have implicated him in a murder, but it's being hushed up on National Security grounds, and because this guy's connected to MI5, Gant'll just sail away into the fucking sunset with no likelihood he'll ever do a minute's prison time. He gets away with it. You know about this case, don't you?"

"Not the whole thing but," he paused and almost smiled at me, "enough to see why things happened as they did."

"And you're comfortable with that?" I asked. "Two men being killed like that to save some bitch's face doesn't bother you?"

Dennison looked at me as if I were stupid and needing to be taught some reality lessons.

"That's what we do, pal. Why do you think I quit the police? I was sick of pulling people in, only to see some fucking lawyer making up sob stories about their client's human rights being violated and them getting away with it when I knew they were guilty as fuck. At least, working here, I know for a fact certain people who deserve to die have done so. You talk about justice. It works differently in different situations. It's contextual. Since I've been here, nobody's died who didn't deserve to. We're on the same side, Rob. You probably don't believe that just now, but we are."

"You think so, eh?"

"Yeah, I do."

I turned and walked away.

Lightning Source UK Ltd.
Milton Keynes UK
UKOW02f0802080515

251135UK00001B/5/P